TOO CLOSE

G Logan

ISBN: 978-1-7370676-0-3 (Paperback)

Cover Art by Jeff "Coom Coom" Coomer

Editing and Layout by Ellen Gehring

To request permissions, contact the publisher at
glogantheauthor@gmail.com

Printed by Lulu.com in the USA.

PRELUDE

Concealed amongst the congestion of cars in the grocery store parking lot, Mitch is eagerly waiting on a new plug to pull up at any moment. "What the fuck is taking him so long?" Watching three cars pass by slowly. None of them matching the description of the car he was waiting for. "This is exactly why I don't like fucking with new people." Complaining to himself as he dials a number on his phone. "Yo, Dan! What the fuck is up with your boy? He got me out here with all this money looking like a target." Spazzing on the phone.

"He's only seven minutes late!" Dan's voice comes through equally agitated.

"Look, Dan, you know how I operate. And with that being said, you know how I don't operate. And this my friend is a great example of how I don't operate." Mitch says in a solemn tone. "My better mind is telling me to roll out and fuck meeting up with your people. He ain't the last person out here that's got a good product. I'm just dealing with him because you say he's your man." Scanning the parking lot for any suspicious faces.

"Well before you leave. Let me hit his line and see where he's at and I'm going to hit you right back."

Noticing the blue Audi, he was described. "No need. I think this is him pulling in now"

"You have to learn to be a little more patient. Everything doesn't happen according to your plans." Dan scoffs.

"My money damn sure will." Grabbing the bag of money off the passenger seat and dropping it to the floor. "I'm going to hit you when I get to the house." Mitch leans forward and signals for Dan's friend to come to his car.

"What's up? I'm Leon, and you're Mitch, right?" Reaching his hand out to greet Mitch.

"We're running late so excuse my need to rush things along." Pointing down to the floor. "That's the money in the bag right there." Reaching out for the bag Leon was holding. "I assume that's for me?"

Leon lifted the bag from the floor as if he were weighing it. Then sat it in his lap and unzipped it to look inside. “Thirty thousand, right?”

“Thirty-two, to be exact. You can thank me later.” Tossing the bag of dope in the back seat. “Next time be on time cause I’m going to have my tip separate. In this game, if you’re late you’re left. Ten minutes can end up being ten years of your life you can’t get back. And I don't have that to waste.” reaching out to shake his hand. “I hope you feel what I’m saying.”

“Dan told me all about how you move.” Receiving Mitch’s handshake. “That’s my fault today. It won’t happen again.” Getting out of the car. “Just hit me when you need me. I’ll be around.”

“That’ll be real soon if this is that pure.” Assured Mitch.

“Oh, you can believe that you’ll be the first to step on it.” Leon closes the door and returns to his car.

As Mitch is riding down Mahoning Avenue, he notices a police car about six cars back “Man not today!” Turning left on Hall Street he accelerated quickly, looking in his rearview mirror. “Whew!” Seeing the police car pass the street. “Thank God!” Making a right onto North Park Avenue he notices an unmarked detective car making the same right. “Oh, y'all think y'all slick.” He mumbles under his breath as he reaches in the backseat and grabs the bag of drugs. “Goddammit!” Mitch slowed down and pulled over, after seeing the unmarked car light up. “Not today motherfucker. Not today.” Stuffing his cell phone in his pocket.

The officer got out of his car and slowly approached Mitch’s car. Placing his hand on his service piece, he stops at the rear bumper of Mitch’s car. “Let me see your hands!” The officer yelled to Mitch. Hearing a motorcycle’s engine revving loud close behind him he turns to see it about to hit him, so he dives out of the way.

The motorcycle stops right next to Mitch’s door. “C’mon!” Rodney’s voice comes from under the helmet.

Mitch jumps out of his car and hops on the back of the motorcycle. “Go! Go! Go!” Holding on tight as they popped a wheelie and sped off. “Whooo!” Noticing they totally smoked the officer after a few turns into the neighborhood. “Pull behind that house.” Mitch hopped off the motorcycle when they got behind the house and opened the shed door. “Put your bike in here.” After getting the bike put up. “I’m going to have my people come get your bike next week and paint it so give me a color and I’ll let you ride one of mine until we get yours back.” putting his hand on Rodney’s shoulder. “I really appreciate you sticking to the script and not bitching out on me.”

“I was starting to wonder if you were paying me for nothing. What’s this, like our thirtieth trip? All I do is follow you home and drive off after ten minutes of watching your street.” Showing a big smile. “I ain’t saying it’s good you got pulled over. But I’m just glad I got to play my part.”

“Well, your part isn’t over yet. What did you see when I pulled off?” Questioned Mitch.

“Man, you ain’t going to believe this when I tell you.” Looking towards the street. “So right after you left, the dude in the Audi got in his car then that car that pulled you over pulled up and he gave that motherfucker some sort of baseball signal.” Tapping Mitch on the arm. “But that ain’t even the crazy part.”

“Well get to it!” Getting impatient.

“Right when I was about to pull off, I saw your boy Dan pull up on him and these motherfuckers saluted each other.” Putting his hand up to God.

“Dan?” Mitch asked, confused. “That motherfucker set me up! I knew that shit wasn’t feeling right! I was only there because he said he couldn’t make it and he really didn’t want to miss that shit! I got his ass now!” Biting his lip in rage. “First let’s get this dope someplace safe. I’m going to grab the keys to that car and have you drive me a couple of places.” Grabbing his head. “I can’t drive right now. I just need to think.” Walking towards the house. “That was too close!”

CHAPTER 1

"What the fuck you mean he got away?" Dan yells into his phone to Leon. "I fucking seasoned the food. Cooked the food. And prepared the plates. All y'all had to do was eat. And y'all let the meal get away?" Trying to calm himself down. "He's not stupid. He's definitely going to know it was a setup! Now I have to figure out another way to get him. It's never going to be that easy again!" Dan hangs up and sparks a cigarette. "Let me see." Scrolling through his contacts while he sits at a red light. "Hell yeah! That's it!" Dialing a number. "Passion, what's up? This is Dan. I got a job for you."

"I know who this is. So that's what we are now? Employer and employee?" Disdainful. "Well, how much are you paying?"

"First of all, you need to stop it with all the attitude. You know what you mean to me. And you know that I am busy." Letting out a sigh. "The job is paying five thousand dollars. Can I count on you or not?"

Speaking in her sweetest tone. "Now you know you can always count on me, like a calculator. I just wish that the same was reciprocated on your end." Looking down at her freshly manicured nails. "So, who's the unlucky guy and when do you need me?"

"Who it is, is a long story. But I need to get you here asap, so I'm transferring half of it to your bank account now and I'll give you the rest when the job is done. I'm going to get you a hotel room for the week, so you can have somewhere to lay until we handle this business."

"Since when do I stay in hotel rooms when I come to see you?"

Trying not to show the stress in his voice. "Look baby, this shit is bigger than our usual work. I have a lot to explain to you when you get here. I can't do all this chatting on the phone. Please just get here."

Seeing how short he was being with her. "This is going against my better judgment but I'm going to do this for you. Just text me the info where I'm going to meet you at." Looking at herself in the mirror. “Give me like five hours cause I have to get some things together around here before I roll out.”

“No problem. Just don’t bullshit me on this. You’re all I got.” Dan hangs up and shakes his fist in celebration. “This motherfucker ain’t going to know what hit him.” After getting a room at a high-end hotel so he’d be ready for Passion’s arrival he falls asleep on the bed.

Passion rubbed Dan’s cheek with the back of her hand. “Wake up sleepy head.” Dropping her dress to the floor. “I know I didn’t come all the way out here to watch you sleep.”

Dan focuses his eyes to see Passion’s curvy figure in her sexy bra and thong set. “Damn baby. I didn’t even hear you come in here. What time is it?”

“It’s time for you to handle your business on this needy little kitty.” Climbing on top of Dan’s chest and pulling her panties to the side to expose her shaved lips. “So, you’re not going to kiss me after all these weeks? These random bitches really making you not miss me?” Sassily.

Without giving it any thought Dan began stroking her mound with his tongue. “You know you’re always my number one.” Sucking and slurping her to a quivering orgasm. “I've been thinking about you every day.” Dan flips Passion over onto her back and begins to plow into her vigorously until he cums inside of her.”

“You’re always trying to leave your kids in me. You know I hate that.” Jumping up to go in the bathroom. “But you don’t want to claim me as your girl. Let me get pregnant and you’re not going to have a choice. Me and Junior are going to be at your house every day. And I dare one of your little floozies to come over.”

“Girl you really are crazy.” Dan snickered. “I don’t know what I’m going to do with you.” Raising his voice as he sees her closing the bathroom door. “Ain’t you still taking your birth control?”

Peeking her head out the door. “Don’t you think it would be a little late to ask that question after you already put your DNA all inside of me?” Closing the door before Dan could respond.

“Just hurry up in there, so I can go over some things with you before I head out.” Buckling his pants.

Coming out of the bathroom. "So, you just waited here to sex me up and now you're leaving? I thought at least, you would give me the first night." Pushing him in his forehead. "I swear, you get on my nerves."

"Listen I never said I wasn't going to come back but I just got a few things to do before it gets too late." Standing to his feet to wrap his arms around her body. "I told you I needed you for some real shit, so you can't just be riding around the city with me for all to see. Now I brought you to this hotel because Warren is literally right up the street, so you can be where I need you to be fast. And you're still ducked off enough, that you're off the radar while you're here chillin. I really need your head in the game on this one." Rubbing the tip of her nose before kissing her. "After this is over, we can go somewhere and spend a few days together relaxing and treating each other special."

"I always treat you special. You always treat me like I'm just another bitch on the team." Pushing him away and sitting on the edge of the bed. "I don't know what I have to do for you to see that I'm really down for you."

"You sound crazy. The only reason I called you is that I know you're down for me. Now, you know the lifestyle I live so you know why I can't be this Mr. Right that you want me to be." Sitting down next to her. "If I had to choose who I'd want to settle down with. It would be you by far. I don't know what you think I'm doing out here, but I don't be out here just laying around with a bunch of different broads. I be out here getting my money. And with that being said. You know my partner Mitch, I told you about?"

"I know by your stories, but I still never met him before. You just always said that's your ace, and since you don't talk about anybody else like that, I figured that's like your right hand or something."

Nodding his head in agreement. "Yeah, he was last week. But this week he's been out here trying to take me out." Looking bothered. "The last straw was the other day when he had me make a move for him and it was an undercover." Clenching his fist in rage. "That was my motherfucking dawg! I've killed people for this dude. And he fucking betrayed me." Running his thumb across his throat. "He's gotta go. You get him to the location I tell you and I'm going to splash him. Simple as that. Problem solved."

"What the fuck you got me in Dan? This is starting to sound like more trouble than you're paying me for."

"Don't worry about nothing. I wouldn't put you in harm's way." Stroking her hair. "I just want you to seduce his ass into taking you on a date and let me take it from there. Look babe, if you don't trust me, keep the twenty-five I sent you and just go back home. I'll figure this out on my own." Turning to walk out the door.

"Wait dumb ass!" Grabbing the back of his shirt. "I told you I was going to have your back and I do. Just make sure this is what you want to do before we go too far."

"We've already gone too far. You're here. And let's be crystal about this. I don't want to kill my best friend. But I know this man. And when I say he is the most calculated and precise person I've ever met in my life." Distress in his eyes. "I have to kill my best friend."

CHAPTER 2

"Today has been one hell of a day," Mitch says to Rodney as he points for him to pull into a driveway. "I really put my trust in you for a situation like today, and I'm happy you rose to the occasion. Now with that being said you know everything's gotta change now."

"I figured that much," Rodney stated. "Just let me know what you need me to do, and I got you, bro."

Paranoid, looking around. "First of all, don't ever tell anyone about this place or my cousin in it. Nobody!" Looking sternly at Rodney. "Just like nobody knew about you. Nobody knows about him."

"I got you, bro. I've been holding down every other secret you've asked me to. I feel like my whole relationship with you is on some secret agent-type shit." Chuckling.

"Well, he's more important than anything I've ever trusted you with."

"Is he crippled?" Pointing at the ramp along the front of the house.

"What, you got a thing against people in wheelchairs? Sounds a bit racist to me." Struggling to keep a straight face.

"Hell no! What type of shit is that?" Flustered.

"Well, we're about to go up in here. And I'm going to need you to put your stereotypes aside." Getting out of the car.

"You know my nephews in a wheelchair?" Authenticating his statement.

"Cuz, it's me. Don't shoot!" Mitch shouts out before he walks in the door.

"I know who it is, I'm just wondering why you have Rodney with you?" Elijah's voice came from the back room.

"What the fuck? How does he know my name?" Whispers Rodney.

"Because I know everything." Shouts Elijah. "Y'all can come back to the lab."

"Yo! I knew I was on some Undercover spy shit!" Seeing Elijah in his wheelchair surrounded by tables, lined with computer monitors. "What y'all really got going on? I thought we were just drug dealers but y'all on some next-level shit for real!"

"Yo, calm down soldier. This ain't what you think. This is just my world. I'm into knowledge. Knowledge is power. And I'm Elijah." Extending his hand to shake Rodney's.

Feeling Elijah's firm grip. "So, skip all that. How did you know my name?"

"Well let's just say that before my cousin goes through with any type of decision of dealing with anybody…" Clears his throat. "He comes to me and I run, what I like to call, a social background search to see what they're all about." Elijah types something on his keyboard and turns his monitor so Rodney could see it. "That's you and your nephew, right? His name is Joshua. His mom, who is your elder sister, Tina. She had a situation with her boyfriend that ended with her in a coma, her son paralyzed and, in a wheelchair, and you locked up with a homicide charge. When you got out, two days later you got approached by Mitch and life has been sweet ever since." Typing something else in. "This is your sister's GoFundMe. An anonymous donor left two hundred thousand dollars. His surgery was one hundred twenty-five thousand dollars. Let's just say you're the one person Mitch put around himself, because of me. I hope this doesn't upset you but when I saw you on the news, I said to myself. That's a real loyal dude right there. We're gonna make sure he's straight. And ever since Mitch met you, he said the same thing. And now here we are. I'm sorry if this all seems a little weird but my whole life has been weird."

"Nah. This ain't weird. This shit might be the realest secret I found out in my life. I just want to say I appreciate you from the bottom of my heart. That money saved my nephew's life."

Interrupting him. "I didn't do it for your praise. And I didn't tell you now for your praise either. I just felt that I'd use the truth to answer your question."

"So how did you get in a wheelchair?"

"Well, that's a long story let me see if I can make it simple." Scratching his head as if he were thinking. "See… I slid to the edge of my bed. Then I put my hands on my wheelchair."

"HaHa, very funny." Taking a seat. "Really. You know my story. Tell me yours."

"I'm going in here to make me something to eat. This guy is about to tell you a movie." Mitch laughed as he walked off. "Y'all hungry?"

"Hell yeah."

"Make me whatever you make yourself but leave mine in the oven. I'm going to eat it later." Directing his attention back to Rodney. "So, you say you want to hear my story. So, I'm really from Virginia. And we had this little beef between the neighborhoods. I wasn't involved in any of it at all but whenever my little cousin would bring his badass down there for the summers, he always had a way to have us with all the bad kids. This particular summer we had a block party, and Mitch begged my mom to let me take him so now I'm forced." Mitch visualized the evening in his head as he told the story.

"You act like you're mad because you gotta go have fun." A young Mitch taunted his big cousin Elijah.

"I just don't want to be out here. They always have too much going on. It's always somebody fighting."

"You act like you can't fight. What are you scared of?"

"Boy you know I ain't scared of nothing." Checking out his clothes one more time before walking up to the party.

"Oh my God! There are so many people out here!" Mitch screamed in amazement.

"Man calm down. These are all the same people we see every day. They're just all in one place so it seems like something big. Look, there goes Shawn and Kenny over there." Pointing across the street at their friends. "C'mon." Motioning for Mitch to follow.

"What's up y'all? I told you we were going to be here." Bragged Mitch as he did the neighborhood handshake with their friends.

Shawn smiles, exposing his missing tooth. "I'm glad you're here. This dude don't ever come outside when you're not here." Tapping Kenny. "Yo, ain't that Robbie and his fuckboy cousins?"

"Hell yeah. That's him with Chris and Mark's ugly asses. That nigga must think you're soft or something. He knows you live on this street. Just let me know how you want to handle it."

"Fuck it! What's up? Y'all down?" Shawn grilled Elijah.

Before Elijah could respond Mitch blurted out. “You know we’re always down to ride. Let’s go.”

“See that’s why you’re my guy,” Kenny said as he began walking. “Most little dudes would be scared to put in that work. You’re always ready.”

Noticing the anger in Elijah’s face. “Or maybe we should see who else out here first.” Mitch tried to backstep.

“I don’t care who’s out here. I’m hitting this dude.” Shawn says before running across the parking lot and stealing on Robbie. “You thought I was just gonna let you walk down my block?” Slamming him to the ground.

“Get off of him!” Kenny says as he punches Mark, for trying to grab Shawn.

Mitch followed up with Chris but being that he was so much younger and smaller he got thrown to the ground immediately. “No, you don’t” Elijah punched Chris in the face and lifted him over his head, slamming him down on the back of his head, knocking him unconscious.

“Bitch!” Mitch rose to his feet and kicked Chris in the stomach.

Pow! Pow! Pow! “Get up let’s go!” Kenny grabbed Shawn from off of Robbie. “C’mon before you get shot!”

Mitch sees his friends run off. “C’mon Elijah!” Mitch notices him slowly walking away and grabs his arm. “What are you doing?” Feeling Elijah falling over. “Somebody help me! They shot my cousin!” Noticing the blood running from Elijah’s body. “I’m sorry cuz.” Holding him tight. “Don’t die cuz. I’m going to fix this.” Sobbing. “I swear I’m going to fix this.”

“And that’s my story,” Elijah says to Rodney.

“So, you mean to tell me that Mitch got you shot? Then what made you move to Ohio?”

“Well, I had fallen into an ultimate state of depression a few years later trying to do my grown man thing. It just seemed like anything I tried, ever worked out for me and Mitch told me he needed some things put in my name since I had good credit. One house led to another house. One favor led to another favor. And next thing you know he bought me this house and asked me to move here permanently and help him out and the rest is history.”

"So, you weren't mad at him for you being in a wheelchair?" Asked Rodney.

"Honestly, I've never been the type to hold anger at a person. I've always believed that things are going to happen, and you're either going to get better or you're going to get bitter. I, myself… I'm gonna get better after anything life throws at me. There's something to learn from every experience."

Noticing the Hebrew pictures on the wall. "Is that why you're so into all this Bible stuff?"

"Not at all. My mother always told me that she named me after a very important person in the Bible and the only way I would understand the meaning of my name was to read the Bible from the beginning to the end. After I got to the Prophet Elijah and saw how he lived and left without dying. I was so intrigued that I was studying the Bible all day every day until I understood that we as the black man are the only people in the world to live up to the Deuteronomy curses, therefore makes us God's chosen people. Which also makes the Bible our history book before slavery."

"So, you did all that studying as a kid off of what your mom said?"

Letting out a snort. "You think that's something. You should've heard some of the shit she told me to get me to read all the encyclopedias."

"The food is done. I made us some burgers and fries." Sliding past Rodney to sit down. "You gotta put your burger together for yourself. I did my part. I left everything you may need on the counter."

"Good lookin bro. I was so hungry it felt like my stomach was eating my back." Rodney wasted no time getting to the kitchen.

"You know I'm still sorry about that day." Mitch expressed solemnly. "I always tell my girl she gotta help me to take over the world, so we can give it to you."

"Look. This shit bigger than me and your plan. This was God's plan."

"What makes you say that?" Questioned Mitch.

"Because if it didn't happen God knew I would've used my good legs to get as far away from you and this hood shit as I could, and he didn't think it was a good idea for your impulsive ass to live without me." Explained Elijah.

"I swear, you got a weird way to see things. But I'm glad for that." Looking down the hall to see Rodney. "Stay out there for a second so I can politic with my cousin about a few things, then we're gonna hit the road."

"I know y'all came on some hot shit, so if you need to stay till the morning, you know you're more than welcome."

"I know cuz, and I appreciate it, but I just needed to get out of the way for a minute to clear my head and make a couple of calls. I still got a few more moves to make in the city before the nights out. But before I go let me tell you about earlier."

"What happened?"

"Well, first of all, I know you heard about a motorcycle chase in Warren earlier, right?" Asked Mitch.

"Absolutely not. I think that's something I would've remembered. So, what about it?"

"Long story even longer. Dan set me up earlier. He had me meet up with his new plug and next thing you know I'm getting run down on."

"So how do you know Dan set you up?"

"I had Rodney sitting back off in the cut watching the whole thing go down. You know how I move. If it wasn't for me being too paranoid today, I would've been locked up." Irritated by Elijah focusing on his computer. "I'm trying to tell you some real shit. What the fuck are you on your computer pecking about?"

"I think that was a hit earlier." Turning his monitor to face Mitch. "Nothing came through the scanner. And trust me. I've been listening to it all day. Which means he didn't call for backup. And I checked the database for a warrant for your arrest and there isn't one which means he couldn't have turned it in. Because if you fled and got away but they had your name you would've had a warrant, put out immediately. I hate to say it, but it looks to me like if you didn't get out of there, they were going to murder you and make it look like something else."

"So, what do you think I should do?"

"Stay low until we figure out what type of shit he's on."

CHAPTER 3

"So, you mean to tell me that all this happened yesterday right after you left me?" Debbie stood up from the kitchen table trying to process everything Mitch has told her. "And didn't I keep saying to you… Baby something don't seem right? I mean he's never had you meet up with his plug without him before."

"And that's how he sold me on it. He was like. You know I wouldn't let anybody meet my plug without me being there. You know I gotta fuck with you bro." Mocking Dan's voice. "It's my out-of-town connection. I told him if he wanted to wait till Friday to meet you that I could be there. He insisted on Wednesday." Mocking Dan's mannerism. "Who else would I trust to have my connect come out with that much dope? You know you're my boy."

Debbie slumped over in laughter. "You sound just like him. That's crazy."

"But for real though. The crazy part is after everything was over I went over Elijah's to see if he might've heard something, about a warrant on me so I would know how to move. And he tells me that nothing came across the scanner, and no warrant was issued."

Looking baffled. "So ain't that a good thing?"

"Yeah, for all those involved in covering up my murder! Why else would all that happen under the radar? C'mon, you know how it is around here. If you get pulled over for a taillight, there's gonna be at least three cop cars on the scene in a matter of seconds. And you mean to tell me that he pulled me, hand on his ratchet." Obviously nervous. "And he didn't call anything in." Giving her a look as to say… Do you get it? "And of all times, he asked me to float the money for his part till he got back from out of town. And he was in the parking lot, the whole time when everything happened." Calculating the details. "So, he was pretty much robbing me for my cash, and the dope was probably part for the dirty cop and part to set me up." Gripping his head. "This shit is fucking crazy!"

"So why do you think he became so bitter at you?"

"I guess jealousy is a hell of a drug."

"Well, if they tried to kill you once, who's to say they won't try again?" Gaping her mouth to gasp. "I got to get the fuck out of this house. You're gonna have me in here getting shot the fuck up!"

Firmly grabbing Debbie's arms and holding her still. "Please calm the fuck down! You know I ain't about to let nothing happen to you. I want you to pack up a couple of things and go to the Cortland property. It's still fully furnished from the open house, and nobody knows about it. Take some time off work and just relax while I take care of things."

Pulling him close to her. "Baby, you better be careful. I swear I'll go crazy if anything were to happen to you."

"You know I'm always careful. I am going to be extra careful with the sharp knives that I'm going to use to chop his body up before burying it in a shallow grave in the woods."

"Well, you know where I'm at if you need someone to help you hide a body." In a seductive voice.

"Don't threaten me with a good time and then try to back out." Kissing her lips.

"Have I ever?" Kissing him back. "But why would he be so jealous, and he's got a lot of money too?"

"Yeah, but when you pull up in a clean ass S Class and think you shut shit down. Then somebody pulls next to you in a Maserati with screens everywhere and makes your little Benz look cheap. I guess that's when you realize that the big shit you've been doing wasn't so big after all."

"You're horrible." Looking in the fridge. "You want me to whip up some breakfast?"

"That sounds good." Getting back to the topic. "So please do me a favor and no new friends. I know that he knows that I know and I'm not trying to take any chances on how he's prepared to try to get at me. All I know is I'm going to be ready and when everything's over, he's gonna be dead!"

"You know you don't have to worry about that with me. I barely hang out with my old friends." Reassured Debbie. "You keep my life interesting enough with all your shenanigans. Plus, we're in Warren. How many new friends do you think are really out there?"

“It doesn't necessarily have to be a stranger. Somebody you’ve known for a long time, but don't hang out with will set you up for a stack. Trust me.” Wipes the moisture from his lips. “If you have any kind of bond with anyone it can be broken. The most dangerous person to break bonds with ain’t your enemy. Y’alls bond keeps y’all apart which keeps you safe. But someone close to you. When bonds get broke, they’re already behind your enemy line.” Takes a seat and signals Debbie to sit. “Look babe, you know in the life I live I’ve seen some pretty fucked up shit. Especially fucking with Dan’s grimy ass. I swear you couldn’t imagine how fucked up he is.” Glancing the room. “What I’m about to tell you stays at this table. If it got out it would be catastrophic. Not only for Dan but for me as well.

“When have I ever said something you said, to anybody?” Rollin her eyes. “C’mon now. You know me better than that. Being with you is like working as a government official. Everything is classified.” Jokes Debbie.

“I swear somebody just told me damn near the same thing. Am I really that bad?”

“Worse.” Taunts Debbie.

“Damn, damn, damn.” Shaking his head. “Let me finish briefing you on our opposition. Do you remember Tyler?”

“Yeah. He used to run with you and Dan. Then he died from an overdose.”

“So, the part that you don’t know is he was Rome’s little brother.”

“You mean y’alls plug, Rome?”

“Exactly. So, they got different moms, obviously. And Rome used to come through and break bread with him all the time to keep him from stealing from people. Even though, that didn’t help. He started fucking up the re-up money, and Rome would cut him off. So, in a roundabout way, he would be cutting us off at the same time. Dan would be so mad when he couldn’t re-up, that one day he approached Tyler’s mom.” Daydreaming the encounter as he speaks.

“Yo, Ms. Sarah.” Dan catches her attention before she enters her apartment.

“What do you want Dan?” Snapped Sarah.

“Is Tyler in the house?”

Sarah puts her head in the door. “Tyler! Are you in here?” Letting the screen door close.

“He ain’t in here. When you see my big-headed son, can you tell him to bring his mom a couple of dollars?”

“What do you need?” Pulling out a wad of money and peeling off a fifty-dollar bill. “And before you say you got me back, I want you to know that you don’t owe me nothing.” Catches his thoughts. “As a matter of fact, can you do me a favor?”

Looking at the crisp fifty in her hand. “Sure.”

Pulling a bag of weed out of his pocket. “I know earlier, Tyler couldn’t find no weed. That’s why I slid past. I ran into some super loud and wanted to bring him a bag.” Letting out a snicker. “Shit. You know he always talks shit about you never looking out for him. Tell him you bought him the bag from someone out the hood. And that he owes you big. You know. Take some leverage back.”

Grinning. “You know, that doesn't sound half bad. Maybe I can get him to clean up his funky ass room for a change.” Speaking in almost a whisper. “Do you have anything else on you? You know? That shit I like?”

“Nah but I’ll bring you something back. Give me like thirty minutes. And if you see him before I do. Don’t tell him you saw me.” Turning his attention to Mitch, who had been standing close by. “You still gonna walk with me to my aunt's house?”

“I got you, bro.” Mitch watches Sarah walk into the house and close her door. “What the fuck was that about? We just left Tyler ten minutes ago.”

Nonchalantly. “Don’t stress it dawg. You’ll thank me later.”

“See. Whenever you say some shit like that. I never thank you later.”

Interrupting Mitch’s story. “Okay. So, he’s shystie because he gave his mom his bag? I don’t get the point.”

“That’s because I didn’t get to the point yet.” Snapped Mitch.

“You're the type of person they made the rule for. Save all questions until the end of the lecture. Now can I get to the point before I lose what I was saying?” Regrouping his thoughts. “We went to Dan’s house, and he picked up some dope, and then we went back to Parker’s, where we saw Tyler earlier. I still didn’t put two and two together, but he told Tyler that his mom was looking for him and that we would walk with him back to his house and chill for a little bit."

"Bro you need to tighten up. You got the best plug in the city, and you be fucking up like that shit don't matter." Dan said, following Tyler into his house.

"I'm with Dan on that one. Every time you fuck up, he starves you which starves us." concurred Mitch.

"Man, I don't give a fuck about that shit! That nigga be trying to act like he's God or something." Tyler spoke out in rage. "Y'all just don't know how he is." Sticking his chest out to mimic Rome's posture. "I put the food on the spoon motherfucker! All you gotta do is eat! Get your foot out your ass and sell some dope!" Laughing at his improv. "I'm just tired of his shit."

"Well, I didn't hear nothing wrong with what he says to you. Hence. That's why we're having this conversation in the first place. You need to just bow out and give me and Mitch the plug."

"We'll show you how to move work." Agreed Mitch as he nudged Tyler.

"I tried to put him on to y'all. He always says… Why the fuck do I have to run business here when I got you here. Trust me. I don't even want to be in the game."

"I knew I heard y'all down here," Sarah says as she enters the kitchen. "What y'all talking about anyways?"

"We are just trying to get your son to get his head on making money instead of chasing these dirty little hood rats around all the time."

"Well, I hope he listens to y'all better than he listens to me because I swear, I'm always trying to tell him that." Sarah pulls a bag of weed out of her bra. "By the way. One of them little boys was trying to sell some weed earlier. He said it was gas or whatever y'all be calling it. But anyways I bought you a bag."

Taking the bag and smelling it. "Nah, this really is some gas!" Holding it out for his friends to see. "Shit, I'm about to roll this right now." Tearing the bag open with his teeth and dumping it on the table.

"Hold up!" Slapping her hand down on the table. "I didn't just give that to you for nothing. I want my bathroom upstairs clean, and I want your clothes on your floor picked up." Seeing him not paying her any attention she gives Dan a look as if to say, "Do you still got me?"

Dan smiled and nodded. "It looked like you dropped a bud on the floor bro." Slipping Sarah the dope when he sees Tyler's focus on the floor.

"Make sure you spray down here when you're done. I'm about to go to my room and watch my show." Making her exit.

"Don't be rolling no loose ass blunt neither. I don't want to smoke if it's going to be running to hell the whole time." Checks Mitch

"Shut your ass up. I've been rolling longer than you." Holding his finished product in the air. "It looks like it was bought like this."

"I know you wanna chill and smoke, but I forgot that shit I gotta do for my aunt. We gotta go. You promised you'd help."

Mitch Looking puzzled. "We supposed to do it now?"

"Not now. Like twenty minutes ago." Reaching out to dap Tyler. "I wish I could enjoy that smoke with you. It smells like some killer."

"While he's playing. Blaze that shit up and let me tap it before I go." Suggest Mitch.

"Stop acting like a whop!" Objected Dan. "Let that man enjoy his blunt." Rushing him outside. "I'll buy a bag when we're done, and we'll come back and smoke."

After they walked down the sidewalk a little way. "Alright, now you really gotta tell me what the fuck is going on." Mitch demanded.

"I'm getting rid of the middleman. What the fuck you think is going on."

"And that's when I knew what he had done. He gave him some bad weed." Regret showing in Mitch's eyes in the form of a tear. "What I still didn't know until later was that he also gave his mom some bad dope so they both overdosed simultaneously in different rooms of their house."

"Debbie covered her gaped mouth with her hand. "Oh my God. So, all this time Dan gave them the bad drugs? I am so in shock right now."

"Listen to me." Grabbing her hands. "This conversation doesn't leave this table. Like I said. I'm only telling you so you can understand the Dan that we're dealing with. And its real funny that after all these years of not being able to fuck with my plug, he volunteers his plug to me, and this happens. So just keep your lips tight on that."

"I understand baby. I promise I won't say a word."

"You know it's crazy because Dan approached Rome at his brother's funeral, and he brought us our first package the next morning." Reflecting on their accomplishments. "It's funny how, no matter who dies, money will always find a way to land in the next man's hand and live on.

CHAPTER 4

"Where are you at?" Dan's voice comes through Passion's phone.

"I'm at the mall. Where you told me to be." Agitated. "No, good morning to you. No, I hope you slept well. No, sorry for standing you up last night."

"Stop being so sensitive. I just got a message saying Mitch is in the shoe store at the mall right now. Don't fuck this up."

"You fucked this up already. Remember, you called me here to fix it." Passion hangs up before Dan can respond. "Here goes nothing." Whispering under her breath as she walks into the shoe store. "Excuse me. Are those the latest ones?" Inquiring Mitch about the shoes he was holding.

"Yeah, they just dropped yesterday. I gotta have them." Checking her out. "I'm debating on which color to get."

"I would buy the red and black ones." Grabbing them off the shelf and checking the price. "Although I wouldn't pay two hundred dollars for a pair of shoes. I just think these look the best."

"Well, thanks for the help." Mitch reaches out his hand to shake her hand.

"Passion." Accepting his handshake. "My name is passion."

"I'm Mitch." Looking down at her shoes. "You probably don't have to pay that much for your shoes anyways. You look like you still wear a kid's size."

"I wish. I wear a size seven. One size too big." Letting out a laugh. "These are definitely grown woman feet."

Signaling the store worker. "Hey, my man. Can I get these red and blacks in a size eleven and get her a size seven?"

"Oh no, no, no. You don't have to do that." Putting her hand up to stop the clerk.

"Yes you do, thank you." Shewing him off. "If you hadn't helped me, I might've been standing here confused for hours. It's the least I can do."

"Well, I wasn't expecting to be spending that much on shoes today so thank you." Giving Mitch an innocent smile. "Since you're buying me shoes, you should let me buy you dinner or a drink or something later."

"That sounds nice and all, but I got so much going on that I have to decline."

"Wow. I've never been shot down so politely before. I don't even know how to feel about it." Joked Passion. "I guess I'm just going to go back to my hotel room and cry myself to sleep tonight."

"Why are you staying in a hotel?"

"I'm just in town for a couple of weeks, to move my aunt out of her house and into a nursing home. She's old and so is her house. It kinda gives me the creeps at night to sleep there, so I'd rather stay at a hotel than sleep at her house." Fanning her nose. "I love my aunt and all, but I just can't do it."

"I can understand that. At least you care enough about family to even be here. I think that's the most important thing in the world." Walking towards the register to pay for their shoes. "I wish you all the luck with getting your aunt straight. And nice meeting you again."

"Damn! You really aren't going to ask me for my number or anything. Well, you sure know how to make a girl feel good." Pulling out her phone. "Tell me your number." Typing it in as he said it. "I just sent you a text from my number. Hit me up whenever you get a chance. I've been so bored around here. I don't know anyone."

"You're probably better off not knowing these shystie motherfuckers around here. These dudes will have you set up, somewhere fast. Shit… I live here and I don't even fuck with people here."

"Well fuck with me so I don't accidentally fuck with the wrong person." Walking out of the shoe store with Mitch.

"Check this out. I ain't about to waste your time or mine. I think time is money. And with that being said." Mitch pulled a wad of cash out of his pocket. "I had a great time talking to you today. You seem like a great person." Handing her ten crisp hundred-dollar bills. "I'm not the guy you're looking for. But he better lock you down fast whoever he is." Giving her one last look up and down. "He's going to be one lucky guy." Before turning and walking off.

"What the fuck was that?" Passion questioned herself as she watched Mitch merge into the crowd and disappear. "He really shut me the fuck down." Tucking her money away and pulling out her phone to call Dan. "I don't know what just happened. I swear I had that nigga eating out my hand. He even bought me some shoes and everything. And when it came time to part ways, I shot my shot because he wouldn't shoot his, and this neutered bitch paid me one thousand dollars to leave him alone."

Laughing at Passion. "I told you he was a whole other type of dude. Don't worry. I got a plan B already mapped out."

"Oh, so you doubted me the whole time?"

"I wouldn't say I doubted you. I just knew that this wasn't going to be easy. I still think you're going to get me to him. I just think you're going to have to take a different approach."

Finding herself a seat on a bench down a side hall, away from people walking by. "Well, I guess, this is when you enlighten me."

"You're going to meet his girlfriend and get her to set him up."

"This all just seems like it's going to be so messy. I really hope you know what you're doing." Displaying her uncertainty.

"I'm about to send you some screenshots of me and Mitch's conversations where he told me to go pick up hotel room keys, and that he already had the room booked. Call her and tell her that you're the other bitch and you got messages to prove it."

"That might actually work. I mean if I had a man, which I don't." Being sarcastic. "I would be pissed if a bitch called me with that shit. And had receipts! So where do I tell her I know him from? I can't say here, because I don't know anything about this place."

"You're right. That wouldn't be good. She's a smart one too." Dan got quiet on the phone for a few seconds thinking. "I got it. Say you're from Virginia. He got some family there and he used to take trips there to pick up dope from some guy out Norfolk. As a matter of fact. Say you met him at a concert. That nigga goes to concerts every summer in Virginia. I remember him and her falling out because she said, he never took her with him. So, I know she'll believe it. She doesn't know much about Virginia so you can kind of make some shit up. She'll never know."

Taking a deep breath. "You really are something else. You don't give a fuck about who you hurt or nothing."

Smirking at her remark. "Feelings will get you killed out here. You better have the heart to execute, or you might get executed. Remember… We play chess not checkers." Dan said smugly.

"So that's why you don't really give a fuck about me? I'm trying to play relationship and you're steadily playing chess. And if I'm not mistaken, in chess the queen might be the most useful piece, because she can move in any direction, as many spaces as she wants, but she's just as sacrificial as a pawn if it came down to her and her king." Giggling at herself. "Now I'm starting to understand you."

"Here you go tripping again." Clutching his fist to keep from yelling. "Can we please just handle this business before you get all in your feelings and do something to get us both killed?"

"Just send me the pics and her info and I'm going to hit her up tonight."

"Nah." Plotting it out in his head. "Do it in the morning. That way if you can talk her into meeting up with you, he won't be around."

"How do you know he won't be around?"

"The same way I know everything else about the man's life. He's been my best friend for the past thirteen years. I don't give a fuck about nothing else. That man gets his day started before seven o'clock, every day."

"Well since my boss gave me the night off, you should bring me some weed." Teasing. "I already got a bottle. I just don't know anybody to be walking up, asking someone, you got some weed?"

"Just text me when you get back to your room. You know I got you."

Mumbling under her breath. "I know you got me fucked up." Putting on a big fake smile. "Don't have me waiting all night." Passion hangs up and continues her shopping.

CHAPTER 5

"You're telling me that a female said hi to you in the store. So, you bought her a pair of shoes and paid her a thousand dollars to leave you alone because you thought she was suspect? And you call me weird." Burying his head in his hands in disbelief. "I think paranoia is making you lose your shit." Elijah rolls down the hall towards his lab.

"Fuck you. Ain't nobody losing nothing." Mitch follows Elijah and lays across the chaise in the corner. "You know I've always been paranoid. That's why I've always stayed one step ahead of my enemies." Winking as he pointed his double finger gun at Elijah before blowing off his imaginary barrels.

"You are absolutely delusional." Pecking away at the keyboard. "What did you say her name was again?" Typing it in as Mitch says it. "And you said she was from Columbus?" Pecking continues. "Finest out of seven. Bingo! I think we got ourselves a hit." Rotating his monitor. "And he shoots at the buzzer for the winning basket."

Staring at Passion's Facebook photo. "Damn! I got to hand it to you cuz. You be on your shit. Now find out why the fuck she's here. She claims she has an old aunt that she's down here to help get moved into the nursing home. Her story sounded pretty real. But…"

"But you got me looking her up anyway because you think she's a Russian spy." Laughing at his humor.

"You're always trying to be a comedian, with your corny ass. Just stick to your day job."

"If you didn't pay so well, I'd probably have a joke for that too. I'm not really seeing anything on her Facebook. I'm going to see if she has other social media accounts linked to her email address."

"Damn Edward Snowden! How the fuck you get her whole email address."

"It's not that serious. She put it in her bio." Picking up his reading glasses and positioning them on his face. "Why don't you just relax and let me do what I do."

"I'm going to let you have that one. I'm about to take a nap. This couch is comfortable as fuck."

"It's not a couch. Couches have arms and are sideways. It's a chaise."

Mitch balled a sheet up and placed it under his head. "I bet you bought it in the couch section."

Elijah waved Mitch off and continued his investigation. "Now what secrets are you hiding in plain sight?" Talking to himself under his breath. "I'm going to find it." Peeking around his monitor to see Mitch dozing off.

A couple of hours later Mitch wakes back up to see Elijah still tapping at his keys. "Shit! I'm going to have to pay you overtime." Wiping the drool from off his cheek.

"I'm on a whole other project." Rubbing his hands together. "I did find something on your girl though."

"Oh yeah!" Mitch hopped up and stood behind Elijah to see over his shoulder. "What did you find?"

"Well first of all. Do you notice anything special about this picture that stands out to you?"

Sucking his teeth. "Hell yeah! I see it!"

"What do you see?" Asked Elijah

"Her nipples." In his old man voice. "It must've been cold out that night."

Shaking his head. "I can't believe how you don't see it. Check this out." Elijah pulls another picture on a different screen. "Now do you see it?"

"Dude, that's a picture of me and Dan kicking it in Florida a few years back. You're totally losing me."

"Didn't you say y'all had those hats and jackets made while you were down there?"

Answering slow and confused. "Yeah, but I'm still not getting your point."

"So, you see she's sitting in a car, right?"

"Clearly." Concurred Mitch.

"Well look what's sitting in the back window." Hinted Elijah.

"That motherfucker!" Mitch shouts and bangs his fist on the table.

Elijah Put his hands out to stop his monitors from falling. "Whoa! You better watch my shit!"

"My bad cuz. I knew it though." Straightening out the things that had shifted. "And you thought I was just paranoid tripping. I know everybody in my city and if someone as fine as her even drove through this bitch, I'm going to know. Like that whole old aunt, the story was good and all. But how did you ever visit her and no one in my city ever seen you before." Cracking his knuckles. "So, that's two people in two days. This motherfucker is trying to get me bad. I got his ass though. Tonight, is going to be his last night on this earth. I hope he enjoys it." Cracking a smile. "Him and his little bitch."

"So about him enjoying tonight." Interrupts Elijah. "I already dropped ten stacks on your young boy, to go get the job done."
"How did you even know how to get in touch with him?"
Puzzled.

"You remember when you had me reach out to him the last time you used him, for those Chavez brothers. Well, I did it the same way, as if I were you." Holding up his phone. "You were asleep, so I texted him from your phone, where Dan was at."

"How the fuck do you know where Dan is at?"

"His dumb ass let somebody go live with him in the background. When I text your young boy, he said he was right up the street from there." Letting out a chuckle. "I felt like it was fate."

"I guess I can't be mad at you. I just wish you would've let me know what you were doing." Returning to the chaise.

"Well, you were knocked out, and I didn't want you to miss the opportunity to get that motherfucker." Tapping the side of his head. "And I think a wise man once said… don't be mad, if while you sleep, another man reaches your dreams."

Astonished. "First of all, don't try and use my own quote against me. Secondly when I said that it sounded a whole lot more gangsta."

"Well, I don't know how much more gangsta I could sound after getting a motherfucker whacked. I'm probably, single-handedly, the most gangsta person you ever met in your life and I'm handicap."

Laughing as he spoke. "Damn cuz, I didn't mean to offend you. You know, I know how hard you go. That's why I roll with you." His smile beaming. "No pun intended."

"Fuck you, you big-headed, pitbull in the face ass chump. I played kickball for the Fairhaven Bulldogs. Don't make me roast you."

Laughing hysterically. "You got it cuz. You got it." Grabbing the broom that was leaning against the wall and beginning to sweep. "I can't joke with you. But I'm about to run to the store." Ramming the broom handle through the gaps in Elijah's wheels. "You stay here!" Running out the door.

"You fucker!" Elijah yells at Mitch who he can hear slamming the front door behind himself.

CHAPTER 6

Sitting on the porch looking down the desolate street. "It's boring as fuck out here tonight," Freddie says to his cousin Paul. "I can't wait until next month when I can start getting in the bar."

"Trust me. The bar life ain't all that you think it is. Niggas be bored as fuck in the bar, just like you be bored out here." Hitting his cigar. "Seeing the same drunk ass hoes every day. Watching the same drunk ass niggas fight every weekend." Taking the last puff of his black and mild before flicking the plastic towards the street. "Shit just be stupid for no reason."

Looking at Paul stupefied. "I'm still not hearing the downside. You're just a boring ass motherfucker." Joking.

"Call me what you want, but your ass be right here with my boring ass, having a ball, every day."

"Well, watch and see how that shit changes after next month. You're gonna find me in the bar." Remembering a thought. "On the real, DJ Dank had it rockin' at the bar last night!"

"How the fuck you know it was rocking if you couldn't get in?" Paul argued.

"I was in the parking lot smoking a blunt with Amber. And the whole lot was full, so I knew it had to be packed inside. Plus, she told me it was. And I could hear the music from the car."

With a dumbfounded expression. "I thought you were trying to fuck Tia. Ain't that Amber's little cousin?"

"Exactly! Her little cousin. I'm on to bigger and better things." Looking down at his phone to read a message that was coming through. "Speaking of bigger and better things, I gotta run and make a move real quick. I'll be right back." Freddie jogs around the corner when he notices that he's about to pass Dan sitting in his car backed in a driveway. "What's up, bro?" Nodding his head as he threw up the deuces. "Let me holla at you for a second." Walking up to Dan's driver's door. "Shit, I know you heard I got the good smoke on deck. But I'm trying to get a better plug."

"So, what does that have to do with me?" Leaning down in the window to see Freddie's face clearer. "You know weed ain't my lane."

"I know you don't sell weed. But that doesn't mean you can't have a killer plug. I've smoked the weed you smoke. Nobody around here gets the weed you get. I want that shit. I got my money right." Flashing a roll of money. "So, what's up?"

"I might be able to do something for you. But what's up with your pistol? Is its services still for hire? Cause I might have a job for you."

"Shit, she's always trying to make a dollar." Tapping his belt to show he was packing. "I've been letting her collect unemployment lately cause the money ain't been right to be risking her like that. I've been trying to be a legit businessman. You know, sell a bag here, sell a bag there. But for you, I might consider putting on my justice suit one more time." Posing like a superhero.

"Boy, you funny as hell. Hop in so we can talk better." Dan hits the button to unlock the door.

"Shit, I got this half a blunt left if you want to smoke on something." Slamming the door. "It ain't the shit you be having, but it's the next best thing." Putting flame to the blunt. "So, what's the word big bird?"

"The word is I need Mitch touched. Immediately!" Slapping the wheel.

"I know you ain't talking about the same Mitch you be with."

"What? Is this too heavy for you to handle? I'm just talking business. If it's out of your league I understand. Just keep your lips sealed about it."

"You know my motto… real g's move in silence. I never told and I never fold. Gimme what you got."

"Well first of all, so you don't think I'm on some crazy backstabbing ass nigga shit. Your boy Mitch tried to set me up with the boys and almost had me hemmed up. Luckily I got out on their asses." Pulling out his wad. "So, you know I'm serious. I only got like two thousand on me." Removing the extra four bills to make it an even two thousand. "I'll give you three more when you're done."

Folding the money and stuffing it in his pocket. “Man, I’m sure glad I ran into you today. God knew I needed some extra money. But for real. I got this, but I still need that weed plug.”

“I got you. By the time you get back with me I’m gonna have all that lined up.”

“Over and out captain.” Freddie gets out of the car and walks around the back of it where he removes his gun from his waistline. clutching the gun close to his leg, to keep Dan from noticing it. “Oh, yeah bro.” Signaling Dan to roll his window down. “I forgot to give you something.” Reaching his gun into the window.

“Fuck!” Dan grabs Freddie’s hands and tries to force them back out the window.

Boom! Boom! Boom! “Bitch ass nigga!” Freddie tucks his gun back in his pants and darts through a couple of yards back to his house.

“Yo cuz, are you alright?” Paul asked, standing alert on the porch holding an AR. “I just heard somebody letting off shots.” Inspecting his cousin’s clothes for blood. “And you just left. I was about to circle the block if you didn’t pop up just now.” Hate and evil gleamed through his eyes. “On my momma, I was about to kill everything breathing out there if something happened to you.”

“That was me letting off.” Rushing to get in the house. “Take this and get rid of it for me” Handing over his pistol. “Be careful. It’s got the safety on, but there’s still one in the head.” Pulling off his shirt, walking into the bathroom. “I had to go lay that hoe ass nigga Dan down.” Pouring bleach on his hands. “Got him something sweet too.” Scrubbing up his arms with a brush. “Dig this right. So, boom. This motherfucker was trying to hire me to kill the nigga that hired me to kill him.” Stepping out in the hallway, hands dripping. “Did you hear what I said cuz?”

“Boy, I heard you!” Paul’s voice came from the back room. “I’m back here dropping your shit in the hole.” Walking back out to the hallway towards Freddie. “You know how hard it is to get to the back of that closet. I felt claustrophobic as fuck back there.” Dusting his clothes off. “But you said he tried to hire you to kill somebody, that already hired you, but I don’t even know who that is.” He scoffs. “Shit. I didn’t even know you were out here filling contracts. My little cousin, the hitman." With his hands in the air to depict neon lights. "Got a nice ring to it."

"You got jokes cuz. I'm serious as a motherfucker right now. Check it. Mitch hit me and told me this nigga was snitching. Gave me the nigga's name that Dan used to set him up and everything. And I know he ain't lying because I got a homeboy doing time in Lucasville, that said he got swooped on by the boys right after getting some work off Dan. And what a coincidence, he had this same cornball ass dude with him." Gesturing with his hands. "So fast forward. I'm about to smack Dan's noodles, and this goof ass nigga offers me a chunk of change, to kill Mitch before I even get the burner out. So, since I'm a businessman I gave him his chance to top my previous offer." Holding up a small stack of money. "He even gave me a deposit." Handing Paul five hundred before shoving the rest back in his pocket. "Nonrefundable of course." They both bust out in laughter.

Regaining his composure. "That shit crazy, but what made them niggas both know to get at you for the hit?"

"Oh, yeah. So, about a year and a half ago, do you remember those crazy-ass Spanish twins that had the spot on Oriole?"

"Oriole? I've never heard of that street in my life." Shrugging his shoulders.

"Yes, you have. It's the side street off of Oak, by Highland."

"You mean the alley! Why the fuck you ain't just say the alley!" Flustered. "Don't nobody know the name of that fucking street."

"Well, I do, and you should. You used to walk down that bitch every day to fuck that old ugly ass broad."

"Yeah, and I always called her, that ugly ass broad in the alley. On my momma I did!" Argued Paul.

"You got it. That is, what you used to say. But let me get back to my story. So anyway, do you remember them?"

"How can I forget them? They tried to jump me. Remember?"

"I wasn't trying to bring that up." With a snicker. "But since you do remember, that's what set everything in motion." Noticing the confusion on Paul's face. "It's all going to make sense in a second. So, boom. I was with Mitch and Dan when you called me. I didn't have a strap on me so I asked them if I could pay one of them for theirs. Dan told me, not only would he give me a gun, but he would pay me five thousand dollars if I bodied them niggas. So long story longer. He texted me two days later and had me pick up the money and the gun from some diesel dude in a fresh ass Audi. I think he was crippled because there was a wheelchair in the backseat."

"Who was that?"

"I swear I've never seen this dude in my life. He kind of had a down south accent. Like he ain't from around here. So later that night I went over to the ALLEY." Stressing alley. "Wasn't nobody outside on the street. It just finished storming. So, boom. I saw the twins on the porch, chilling, drunk as fuck." Visualizing that night as he told the story.

"Boy, you almost got yourself shot, pulling up on that bike like that." Eddie Chavez addresses Freddie.

"My bad. I didn't even notice y'all on the porch."

"What you looking for?" Questions Terry Chavez. "We ain't doing no small shit today. Eight balls or better."

"I got you. I was tryna cop a half." Freddie pulled some money out of his pocket all balled up.

"The half is five, but I'll sell you the whole thing for eight right now if you're ready." Bargained Terry.

"I'm just going to wait until next time. I didn't bring that much with me."

"I'll have the same deal for you next time if you don't take too long. Let me run up here and grab that for you." Terry went into the house and closed the door.

"So, I see your little ass, done came up with some cash flow. You were just grabbing flips for fifty last week. I don't know who you robbed, but you better watch your ass out here in these streets. I know you come around here on that hot shit; it's not going to fly at all." Threatened Eddie.

"I didn't rob nobody for shit. I worked hard for this money." Sorting his bills to all face the same direction. "Y'all lucky I'm bringing the money to y'all because I could've easily gone to Mitch and Dan. I just don't want to have the same shit everybody else got. Plus, I heard some whops saying that y'all had some A one yola."

"Boy don't play with me. You know we keep the best. That's why your boys be mad cause we're locking down y'alls city and we ain't even from here. This shit too easy." Reaching down to grab the bottle of liquor, that was sitting next to his chair.

Crack! Freddie hit Eddie in the face with his gun and watched him fall out of his chair to the floor. "Be real quiet or I'm going to splatter your shit." Freddie stood over Eddie and put his finger in front of his mouth to hush him.

"What the fuck?" Terry came out the door.

Boom! Boom! Boom! Freddie shot Terry two times in the chest and Eddie once in the head before he could get to his feet. "Y'all bitch ass niggas ain't taking over shit." Scooping up the dope that fell from Terry's hands before hopping on his bike and pedaling away.

Paul's jaw dropped, mystified by the story. "So, you mean to tell me, this whole time, it was you that killed the Chavez twins?" Still in disbelief.

"I've been trying to tell you to put some respect on my name!" Pulling out his phone. "I'm about to hit Mitch up and let him know the mission is complete. Why don't you roll some of that weed up so I can smoke and calm my nerves?"

"I guess you deserve one after all that."

CHAPTER 7

"Checkmate!" Mitch shouts out as he reads the text that came through his cell. "I gotta hand it to you cuz. You sure know how to put a plan in motion. I was about to give it until tomorrow to figure something out. It's been less than three hours and the job is done." Nodding his head. "I'm impressed."

"Saying you're impressed by me doing exactly what you've always known me to do is a contradictory statement." Adjusting his posture in his wheelchair. "Nobody is impressed when Lebron dunks a basketball. Excited maybe, but not impressed. Impressions are made, the first time you experience something. After that, it either fits the mold or it doesn't."

"You sure know how to ruin a compliment. But now that you put it like that. I'm not impressed." Tilting his head to the side. "Yo, check the cameras. It sounds like somebody's pulling up." Standing up from the chaise. "It's probably Rodney. I told him to pick me up, so I don't have to take my car to the Cortland crib."

"Well pull it to the back because I'm having another chair delivered tomorrow and I don't want my ramp blocked." Seeing Rodney exiting his car on the screen. "Yeah, that's him."

"Do you want me to just park it in the garage?"

"What? On top of your Jaguar?"

"Oh shit! I swear, I forgot I had that thing parked over here. I was supposed to have had that put back up in the storage unit. So, I've been paying them all this time for an empty unit?" Mitch walks towards the front room to answer the door. "I gotta get my shit together. I'm losing whole cars and shit." Mumbling under his breath to himself.

"I didn't come too early, did I?" Rodney asked Mitch upon entering.

"You're right on time." directing with a motion. "Come back to the lab. We were just chopping it up."

"What's up with you?" Rodney greets Elijah. "Y'all back here concocting a world take over scheme? I want in on that deep shit!"

Elijah looks towards Mitch. “You know how we get down. If your feet can touch the bottom, then you haven’t gone deep enough.”

“Big facts!” Agrees Mitch.

“But for real. I was telling this dude that I’m about to get a new chair tomorrow.”

“What’s wrong with that one? Is it broke?”

“Nah this one is more compact for better turns and moving around the house. The one I’m getting tomorrow is more for going long distances. And it’s so much faster.”

“What’s wrong with the chair I gave you in Vegas for your birthday? That was made for long distances.” Confronted Mitch.

“For one, I don’t need all that attention. And on the other hand, when was the last time you saw a diesel paraplegic in an electric wheelchair.” Flexing his huge biceps before putting his wheelchair in a wheelie position. “Electric wheelchairs are for the weak. They were made to make life easier and arms smaller. I’m good using my arms while God still grants me usage of them.”

“Where is this flashy one that y’all talking about?”

“It’s in that closet right next to the bathroom. Where it’s been since we got back from Vegas.” Mitch said sarcastically. “You can check it out.”

Rodney stepped into the hallway and opened the closet door. “Oh shit! This motherfucker fresh as a bitch. I know it’s bad luck, but I wanna ride this shit” Pulling it out to see the wheels. “Are these real gold?”

“Hell yeah! And he got caps that he can put on and they turn his rims into spinners.” Making sure the closet was closed securely after Rodney returned the chair.

“I’m with Mitch on this one. I’d have to ride that bitch somewhere. That’s the dopest wheelchair I've ever seen in my life.”

“I ain’t even gonna lie. I love that chair. But you know what we got going on. I don’t need any extra eyes watching me and wondering what I’m doing. That chair even has speakers built in it that all I have to do is plug my phone up to the auxiliary connection, and I can play anything I want. It’s pretty loud too.”

“That’s crazy. I wanna get something like that for my nephew. I know he’ll ride it.”

"We can put something together for him. Just let me know what all you want on it and my man will make it happen. And I mean anything." Recollecting a thought. "I remember one time I went in his shop, and he was putting a top on a wheelchair, just to put a sunroof in it."

"That's crazy," Rodney says in amazement. "Tell him I want some switches."

"That's eleven hundred." Confirmed Elijah. "And it's really uncomfortable the way it jirates you around. Feels like you're riding a mechanical bull or something."

"Okay scratch the switches. I'll think of some shit and get back with y'all."

"What you got planned for tonight? I might need you to stay at the telly tonight so I can have you close by in the morning. I'm going to have you drop me off at the spot in Cortland."

"I thought you weren't using that house until next year."

"That was the plan. But you know what they say.... plans change." Looking over to Elijah. "I'm just glad that you talked me into sticking to the plan of getting the plumbing job done instead of putting it off till next year."

Boasting. "You always do good when you listen to me. I don't know why it's so hard for you to connect the dots. Every time you go on your vigilante escapes, I have to, in one way or another, help you clean up a mess."

"Look who's crying over spilled milk." Mitch mocked Elijah in a baby voice.

"Spilled milk?" Straightening his posture. "Spilled milk don't cost thousands to cover up. Spilled milk don't take ammonia, a mask, and gloves to clean up." Rolling his eyes in his head.

"Why you getting mad?" Antagonized Mitch.

"Boy, you know you can't make me mad."

Sending a wink at Rodney. "He's mad more than a motherfucker!"

"You two are hilarious." Rodney hunched over holding his stomach. "I swear y'all argue for no reason."

"We argue because he thinks he knows everything." Blamed Mitch.

"No. We argue because he don't know shit, and I know everything." Corrects Elijah.

“Not to change the subject but… if we stay in Cortland tonight, how do you want me to be where I’m supposed to be in the morning?”

“Like I said, plans change. That shit already got handled.” Pointing a finger at Elijah “This motherfucking master of war made that move like an hour ago. So tomorrow we’re just going to lay low, and chill. I don’t know how his little detective friend is going to react to this.”

“Damn. I ain’t even gonna lie. I was kind of looking forward to putting in some work on your boy.” Rodney exposed his gun handle. “I just wanted to make sure I still got it.”

“Trust and believe, if you’re anxious like that, you definitely got it.” Looking stern. “Check it. It’s always better to avoid as much as you can. Because there’s so much of life that’s unavoidable. And if you don’t pick and choose your battles wisely, they will overtake you. And I’m pretty sure you still be having nightmares from your first body. Why force torture on yourself if you don’t have to.”

“I feel you, bro. You haven’t steered me wrong yet.”

“And I don’t intend to. Since when did Batman put Robin in danger?”

“Every episode!” Exclaimed Elijah

“You know what I’m trying to say!” Sticking up his middle finger. “You just gotta be a dick!”

“Rather be a dick than a pussy. Because pussy’s get fucked.” Looking at Mitch with a side-eye. “Or at least I think that’s how it goes.”

“That’s the second time today that you used one of my lines on me. I’m starting to feel like I’m arguing with myself.”

“In a sense you are. Just a better version. Since I taught you everything you know.” Taunted Elijah.

“Dude I’m about to get out of here before you make me put my hands on you.”

“Please grab me.” Flexing his biceps. “I haven’t balled you up in a long time.”

“I let you do that, cause I was trying to boost your confidence.”

“Okay, then grab me and show me it was a hoax. That you let me win, better yet...” Elijah unbuckles his seatbelt and plunges to the floor putting himself in a sitting up position. “I’ll even start from the ground.”

“Jump on him, Mitch.”

“He don’t wanna come down here with me. He knows my groundwork is amazing. I’m liable to choke his ass out.”

“Man, if I didn’t have on my good clothes. You already know what I’d do.”

“Yeah, I know what you’d do. You’d make excuses for me tapping you out again.” Grasping the handle on his wheelchair to pull himself back up. “Boy you know if I get a hold of you with these pythons, there ain’t know getting me off.”

“You win cuz.” Giving him dap. “We’re about to roll out. Call me in the morning if you need help getting your new chair together.”

“I should be good. They usually come pretty much put together. But good looking out.”

“No problem cuz. I’ll be back this way in the early afternoon.”

“Alright, bro.” Rodney gives Elijah a dap before they leave.

CHAPTER 8

A fifteen-year-old Rodney hits a jump shot from the three-point line. “Game! I’m done beating on y’all for today. I’m about to go in and get me something to eat.” Grabbing his backpack off the ground and flinging it over his shoulder.

“You should stay and play one more game.” Berney says dribbling around Rodney.

“Man, I've been out here since this morning balling.” Wiping the sweat on his hands down the front of his pants. “You just got out here an hour ago. I’m done.” Stretching his hands out in front of him. “Throw me my ball.”

Bernie palmed the ball out in front of himself before tossing it to Rodney. “You should let me hold it till tomorrow bro. I don’t like shooting with that other ball. It don’t got no grip.”

“Last time I left my ball with you I almost had to go in my bag to get it back.” Tapping his backpack.

“Nigga, you ain’t about to shoot nothing but the same bottles and trees you’ve been shooting with that little ass pee shooter.”

“Bitch, it wasn’t a pee shooter when them niggas jumped your ass and you was all crying... Let me hold your gun bro.” Mocking Bernie. “I’m going to kill all of them niggas bro.” Seeing he was getting under Bernie’s skin. “I know you’re about to get emotional, so I’ma let you hold it. Don’t get my shit took.”

“I got you. I swear I’ma take it home with me tonight. And that time you’re talking about. I smoked some weed with Tito, and I forgot I even had a ball.” On the defensive.

“We're good.” Rodney walked down the street to the front yard of his apartment where he heard his sister’s voice screaming.

“Leave me alone! I hate you!”

“Fuck!” Rodney ran inside where he could see Tina snatching away from her boyfriend at the top of the stairs. “Yo! Get the fuck off my sister!”

“Get the fuck off of me Tim!” Pushing him in the chest.

“Bitch!” Tim's massive fist covers Tina’s whole face, knocking her unconscious. Seeing her head bounce off the edge of the bookshelf that stood in the hallway, on her way to the floor. "You see what you made me do? I told you I wasn't playing with your ass!"

"Don't hit my Mommy!" Joshua jumped on Tim's back, and Tim flung him over the banister down to the first floor near where Rodney was standing.

"Joshua!" Rodney looked down at his nephew's lifeless body before grabbing his gun out of his bag. "You got me fucked up!" Cocking his gun Rodney charged up the stairs towards Tim. "I should blow your shit off!" Pointing his gun in Tim's face. "Back up!"

"Little nigga. You ain't going to shoot me." Taking a step towards Rodney. "Do you know what'll happen to you? I'll have my dawgs fuck you up all around this bitch!" Easing in slowly with his hands up.

"Back the fuck up!" Pow! Rodney shoots one shot into the wall next to Tim to show his threat was serious. "I'm not playing! Back the fuck up!"

Sensing his fear. "You know you're violating motherfucker. You better put that gun down before this shit gets out of hand." Trying to seize a chance to pounce.

Peeking around the corner to view his sister who had blood running from her head. "You killed my sister!" Looking back at Joshua who was still lifeless as well. "You killed my nephew! I don't give a fuck about what you talking about. This shit already out of hand!" Seeing Tim lunge towards him. Pow! Pow! Pow! Pow! Pow! Click. "AHHHH!" Rodney let out a holler, as he watched Tim fall almost in slow motion, face-first to the floor. "Fucking die!" Dropping to his knees, he crawls to his sister and embraces her crying. "No! No! No! Tina, wake up! Wake up! Slightly shaking her. Realizing she's not going to respond. "I'll be right back." Carefully laying her back down. "I'm going to check on Joshua." Running down the stairs to his nephew's contorted body. "Oh my God!" Rodney took off to the kitchen leaving a trail of vomit all the way to the sink. "What do I do? What do I do?" Squeezing his head from both sides. "Just calm down." Talking to himself.

"I can't move." Joshua's faint voice came into the kitchen. "I can't move."

Rodney darts to the living room, bracing the wall to stop himself from slipping in his own vomit. "I'm right here nephew. Just lay still." Crouching next to him. "I'm going to get you some help. Looking across the room to see Tina's phone on the floor. He scurries over. "What the fuck!" Noticing her phone's screen is shattered, he opens the front door yelling. "Help! Somebody call the ambulance! Please! Somebody help me!" Rodney's phone rings, waking him from his dream. "Oh shit." Focusing his fresh eyes to see Mitch's name on his screen before answering. "What's up, bro?" Clearing his throat. "Is everything okay?" Glancing out the window. "What time is it?"

"Fuck the time. I need you to get up and come meet me ASAP."

"Wait. What?"

"Rodney. I need you to wake the fuck up and hear me!"

"I'm up." Putting the call on speaker and standing to his feet to stretch. Just let me brush this dragon out my mouth and I'm on my way. But you still ain't telling me nothing."

"Plans changed again. Dan's still alive!"

CHAPTER 9

"Good morning sleepy head." Dan says to Passion, noticing her waking up.

"Good morning baby." Wiping the sleep from her eyes. "Have you been staring out that window all night?"

"Yeah. You can never be too careful with this motherfucker. I told you he's calculated as fuck." Holding his arm close to his stomach.

"How's your arm feeling?" Sitting up against the headboard.

"It's crazy because my arm don't hurt that bad. I mean it feels heavy and warm for some reason, but it's not like pain, pain. If you feel what I'm saying."

"Yeah, that could be it trying to get infected. When the drugstore opens, I'm going to go get you some stuff so we can clean it again and wrap it better." Walking over to Dan to examine him more closely. "How's this feel?" Rubbing his stomach.

Cringing. "Now that hurts. Thank God I had that vest on, or I'd be a dead bitch right now. Young boy really tried to take me outta here."

"Yeah, and then who was going to pay me the rest of my money?"

"Damn! That's where you're at now? Fuck me? Just make sure you get paid huh?" Letting out a half-suppressed laugh. "Don't worry. I'm going to make sure you're straight." Shaking his head in contempt as he turned to look back out the window. "I can't get no love in this bitch." Mumbling under his breath.

Responding sharply. "I can hear you talkin shit." Walking into the bathroom. "Don't try to turn this around on me like I haven't been trying to be something real in your life. You always be on your bullshit, so I'm done trying. Be happy with these basic hoes you be fucking with." Fixing her hair in the mirror. "I swear you can't make a motherfucker see what he's got till he sees it with someone else. Then it's like, I want my girl back." Ridiculed Passion. "By then, shit! Your girls gonna know how it feels to be treated by a real man, and she's never coming back."

"You act like I don't treat you right. Every time I'm around you, all we do is shop, get fucked up, and stunt the city. Now all of a sudden I do you so wrong."

Flushing the toilet. "You just don't get it. You might not ever get it. But it's okay. Cause I'm done trying to be what you want. Somebody is going to love all these sexy curves in their bed every night. These voluptuous lips on their dick after a long day's work. Oh, and don't forget I burn it down in the kitchen."

"I'll give it to you. You know the secret to keeping a man's stomach full and his balls empty. But be real with yourself. You like this adventurous lifestyle. All the money it comes with. Designer bags, designer hats, and all that fancy shit you be wearing. You're gonna be bored out of your mind trying to play Susie homemaker." Scofts. "Don't no man want his woman up in the bar every week around a whole bunch of drunk ass niggas."

"Well, if I had a man to stay home with, I probably wouldn't need to go to the bar. But since I don't, I do me. It ain't like I'm taking different dudes' home with me every night. I fucking go home, by myself, and be bored while I see these ugly hoes out here with whole husbands. I swear life ain't fair." Wiping a tear from her face. "Don't nobody wanna settle down with the pretty girl because everybody worried about the next man taking her. When all she wants to do is be happy with one man that cherishes and loves her."

"Well, that's not my reason at all. I've told you a million times. I'm not going to be claiming no one or having no one claiming me when I know I'm too deep in these streets to put someone on a pedestal. I don't have time to be explaining myself to nobody. I do what the fuck I need to do when the fuck I need to do it. As soon as you get in a relationship everybody wants to bring their own set of rules. And I'm not with that."

Disgusted. "You are so stupid. I don't want to talk about this with you anymore. You're really beginning to piss me off."

"You say I'm stupid, but how am I sending you to get my boy?" Not really giving her time to answer. "Through his fucking girl. So, proving my point. It's never a good thing to have someone too close to you in this game because people will use them or hurt them to get to you. I do what I do to keep the people I love safe."

"So, you don't wanna fuck with me because you fuck with me so hard?" Sarcastic. "Yeah, like I said, you're stupid." Angrily picking up trash off the table from last night.

"You just want everything your way. And if it ain't your way, you don't even try to see the vision." Wiping her tears with his finger. "Trust and believe, if Mitch knew about you, you'd probably already be dead or kidnapped by now." Pulling her in with his one good arm. "Mitch thinks that I don't give a fuck about nobody. Which means he's only got me as an option to get me. Which means I'll see it coming. I need you to trust me just one more time. Or none of this is gonna work."

"Well, you got me this time. But I'm going to be honest with you. After this, I'm done. Don't call me again. I don't even wanna work with you no more."

"Damn you're breaking up with me?" Dan asked, confused.

"You have to be in a relationship to break up with someone. I look at us more like business partners. So, it's more like me quitting a job. Boss." Sucking her teeth.

"Man, I ain't hearing all that. You're talking crazy. But I'm gonna let you have that one. Let's just get this job done. And we'll worry about what's gonna happen later when later gets here." Pulling his phone from his pocket and pulling up messages between him and Mitch. "Go through these messages and pick any of them that you think you can manipulate to say he was talking to you and screenshot them and send them to your phone."

"Why can't you do that. You always got me doing the bullshit work."

"I want you to choose your own lies. That way you remember what to say." Assured Dan. "After you get that part together, you're going to call his girl and tell her what you got to say and when she denies that you're telling the truth, send her the screenshots to show his number messaging your number. Oh yeah and tell her your name is Angie. It's a bitch in Virginia that he did holler at one day." Taken aback by his genius. "I don't know why I didn't start with this plan. It's foolproof." Noticing the blood has soaked through his wrapping. "Put that on pause, and redo this for me."

"I'm not a nurse. I don't know why you keep refusing to go to the hospital." Gently unwrapping his wound. "I'm scared it's gonna get infected."

"Don't worry about all that. I got some antibiotics coming to me in a couple of hours. I just gotta keep the wound clean and pressure on it. When we get the rest of the supplies, we're just gonna pack both holes. Where it went in up here." Pointing to the hole. "And where it came out back here." Rubbing his rib. "Man! I swear I'm going to kill that little motherfucker." Bracing himself as he watches her rewrapping his arm. "Don't be scared to go as tight as you can. That's what's gonna keep it from bleeding out."

"If you know so much about wound care, why the fuck are you wasting your time being a drug dealer, instead of being something useful. Like becoming a surgeon or even an ER doctor."

"I'm more useful than both of them. I'm who people come to see when the doctors can't fix what's inside of them. I medicate their souls and their minds."

"You're sick!" Pulling harder on her makeshift wrap. "Oops! I hope that's not too tight."

Wincing in pain. "Bitch!" Pointing at her. "Don't forget, I ain't left-handed. My slap a bitch hand is still active."

"I ain't gonna be too many more of your bitches." Throwing a towel at Dan's face.

"You ain't gonna keep hurting me either." Massaging his arm through the wrap. "Last motherfucker that hurt me…"

"Last motherfucker that hurt you is at home right now, smoking a blunt and drinking some tea, with his young ass. Telling somebody about how he shot the fuck out of your ass." Looking down at Dan's angry face. "Don't play with me."

"You're right." Gripping his beard. "So, what do you say we go get that bitch ass nigga today."

"What do you say, you mention my coin when you address me about business matters." Rubbing her fingers together in the air.

"How's five more sound to you?" coaxed Dan.

"Sounds like we're at seventy-five."

"Damn. I know how to add." Ruffled.

"So how do you wanna approach the young boy?"

“He’s young. You’re sexy as fuck.” Running his hand down her figure. “All you gotta do is pull up. Buy a bag. And he's gonna be so hype when you ask him to match you a blunt, he’s gonna hop his ass in the car. It’ll be more like a volunteer abduction.”

“You sure you don’t want to rest for a couple of days.” Caressing Dan’s shoulders. “And let me take care of you till you feel a little better?”

“I’m sure that I can’t afford to rest, with this motherfucker out here plotting on me. I received his message. Cause that’s all that amateur shit was. But I’m about to send his message back to him in a body bag.” Smiling with a wicked grin. “Go ahead and get those messages out my phone. We got a long day ahead of us.”

CHAPTER 10

"So how did you find out he wasn't dead?" Rodney asked Mitch.

"Shh." Looking around the room. "Debbie doesn't know anything about this, and I don't know if she's up or not. She'll just be laying there listening and then come out later like she had some type of psychic vision or something." Nudging Rodney. "We gotta move anyways. I'll tell you all about it when we get in the car." Opening his bedroom door slowly to peek in on Debbie who was sitting up in the bed. "I knew you were up. What are you in here doing? You're trying to hear what we're talking about, ain't you?"

"No!" Giggling. "I don't care what y'all got going on."

"Yeah right. That's why you're laughing. You know I'm right." leaning down to her. "Kiss me. I'm about to go."

"So much for breakfast in the morning."

"I'm sorry baby. I swear something major came up. I promise I'm gonna make it up to you."

"You always do." Debbie lays back under the covers. "I guess I have more time to rest."

"I'm probably going to be gone until this evening." Walking out. "C'mon man let's go."

As soon as they got in the car, Rodney jumped right back on topic. "So, for real. How'd you find out that nigga ain't dead?"

"How do you think I found out?"

"Elijah? Man, I swear, he's not just good with computers. He is a computer."

"Don't let him hear you say that. He might try and make you his right-hand man." But for real. He called into the hospitals and the morgue, and they all said Dan wasn't there."

Puzzled. "But ain't that what the hospital's supposed to say when somebody gets shot? How do y'all know they ain't lying?"

"That's probably what they're supposed to say in a major city. But right here, in Warren Ohio, they're going to be like I'm sorry sir, but we can't disclose that information to you." In his elderly woman's voice. "And that's how you know."

"So, what's plan B?"

"Plan B is the same as plan A was before there was a change of plans. It's just going to be a little harder to trap him because he's gonna be looking for us to try something else now. He's probably gonna stay ducked off somewhere for a couple of days or something. But trust and believe that as soon as he pops his head out to get some air, we're gonna be on his ass."

Letting out a subtle laugh and then a sigh. "I know you keep saying that this ain't no secret agent man shit that we're on. But if I can be honest. It sure feels like some secret agent shit."

"Well keep your secret agent eyes on the road." Fidgeting to get his seatbelt on.

"How long have I been driving you around? I got this brother. All I need you to do is point me in the right direction."

"Alright smartass. We gotta run back out to Elijah's for a minute. I have to drop off some shit real quick and then we gotta go find Freddie. I've been calling his phone all morning and it just keeps going to his voicemail." Lifting his cap to scratch his head. "I hope his little ass is okay. I, personally, wouldn't have put him on to Dan. But I ain't got nothing to say when I wasn't complaining when I thought he pulled it off. That would be borderline hypocritical."

"I must agree with that. So look bro, I was thinking… not to sound like I'm on some scary type of hoe shit. But you know what I went away for." Glancing over to see if he had Mitch's attention. "I know I was all hyped up to put in work the other day. But the truth of the matter is, that shit from before still haunts me. I don't know if I can handle adding any more demons to the ones I already got." Taking a deep breath. So, I guess what I'm trying to say…"

Interrupting Rodney in mid-sentence. "I get what you're trying to say. You don't gotta say no more. I'm just glad you kept everything one hundred with me from the jump, before anything happened and not just freezing up in action."

"Now maybe you misunderstood me. I was just saying I don't want to be assigned to do any hits. I wasn't saying I'm scared to protect mines in the midst of battle. Trust me. If it comes down to it being one of us or one of them, best believe my gun is gonna bust!" Kissing his two fingers to the sky and crossing his heart.

"The demons that'll haunt me for letting one of my loved ones die on my watch, is probably way worse than the demons I got now. I might as well choose the ones I feel like fighting for the rest of my life"

"Trust me." Looking stony. "I have my share of demons. I just don't talk about what don't need to be explained. Ya, feel me?"

"I feel you completely. But let me ask you a question totally off subject."

"Shoot."

"I know he didn't choose where he was gonna live, so what made you choose to put this nigga in McDonald?"

Mitch laughs and ponders the right words. "You're from Ohio, right?"

"Born and raised."

"How many people do you know from McDonald?"

"One, now that I know Elijah."

"Exactly! Why would I put him somewhere that people I know are just going to randomly ride by and see one of my cars in his driveway? I put him where he could be comfortable. And I know he's safe to move around how he likes to. People on his street love him. You would've thought he was from here for real, the way he interacts with them. And that's the life he wants to live. Not this street shit we do all day. And fuck it. You heard the story about how he got in that wheelchair. It's the least I could do for him."

"So, you really blame yourself for what happened to him?"

"You don't think he does? He wouldn't have even been there if it weren't for me. Let alone been in the fight that got him shot."

"So, when are you going to reach the point to where you feel y'all can be even?"

"In all seriousness bro." Solemnly. "When my cousin can walk again." They both remained silent for the rest of the ride.

CHAPTER 11

Pulling into the gas station, Debbie can see the car Angie had described to her. "Lord, please help me keep it together. Because without you I'm afraid I'm going to rip this little girl's head off. Amen" Pulling up on the side of her. "Park your car over there away from the pumps and get in with me." Eyeing Angie's every move as she gets out of the car. "Damn, she's fucking gorgeous. I know he fucked her." Whispering to herself. "Just breathe. Just breathe." Unlocking the door as Angie approaches. "Hey, girl. You don't mind riding with me while we talk, do you?"

"Nah. I'm just glad you came to meet me by yourself. I didn't want to be fighting with a bunch of ratchets." Fiddling with her hair. "I don't feel like replacing my weave yet."

"Just know I don't go nowhere by myself." Debbie patted her purse. "But I'm way too classy to ever be on any ratchet shit. I don't know what you do, but I'm a boss about everything I do." Examining herself in her visor. "So how is it you say you got with my man?"

"Well, we met in Norfolk, at a concert. He invited me out to have a couple of drinks with him." Sticking to the script.

"Him and who else?" interrogated Debbie.

"It was just him by himself." Looking down at Debbie's purse. "Afterwards, we met up at a bar. He was still by himself, but I had my home girl with me. That stopped nothing. We all got wasted until the bar closed, then we went to the hotel."

"See I know you're lying because he owns houses in Virginia, so why would he take you to a hotel and risk me seeing his credit card statement."

"No, he didn't get a room. Me and my friend already had a room. We were only down there for the concert. That's why I connected with him immediately when he told me he was from Warren. I'm from Columbus, but I used to be down here for the summer as a child. I told him we used to always go to that hot dog spot whenever I was in town. And he was like you've definitely been to Warren." Proud of her performance.

Burning on the inside. "So, you, him, and your cousin all hung out that night?"

"If that's what you want to call it. I caught his signs. He caught my signs. My homegirl even threw some signs. I was like, fuck it girl. We were out of town. We ain't going to never see this dude again. Not knowing at the time, that I was going to fall for him." Looking at Debbie with a sympathetic look on her face. "I'm so sorry. I see this is hard for you to take in by your aura. I'm a Virgo. I can read people. I'm not trying to hurt you. I just feel like I've been his girl for a long time. And you, obviously longer. But I figured that if I found out about you, then maybe you should find out about me."

"So, you came here to make us fall out, in hopes that he would come home to you?"

"Oh, no girl. He's clearly your man. I see him whenever I'm convenient to his schedule. I just felt that all parties involved had the right to know who all was attending the show."

"So what about your friend, is she attending the show? Or does she just pop in when that's convenient?"

"That was just a one-time thing. I explained to him that we don't usually get down like that. It was just some out-of-town wilding out shit."

"So why did you bring me screenshots? Why not just show me the messages on your phone?"

"Well, that's from a whole other phone altogether. He shut it off when I told him that I thought I was pregnant. He said I had to be fucking somebody else because he can't have kids. I gave him that phone back. But before I did, I took a screenshot of all those messages and sent them to my real phone. There's like fifty more if you want to see them." Whipping out her phone.

"I think I've seen enough of y'alls messages. I don't doubt that you can produce messages. But hold up. Back up. What was that last thing you said? You said you thought you were pregnant? So y'all was out here having unprotected sex?"

"Not all like that. He usually used a condom, but it's been those times in the morning or the shower. You know. When you just get caught up in the moment."

Looking over at Angie, trying to hold back her emotions. "And what might I ask, did he say happened to make him not be able to have kids?"

"I don't really remember the full story because we were kind of drunk, but he said something along the lines of he got into a motorcycle accident and had an injury to his groin or something like that. He said he had to wear a diaper for like two or three months." Taking her time to get the details right, just how Dan coached her to.

"Well, it doesn't sound like you can't remember. It sounds like you remember the story quite well. I'm scared to ask you what else you know. I guess what I want to know is what now? What are your true intentions?" Thinking to herself, how real all of this sounded.

"That's up to you. We can go our separate ways, and live the lives we've been living, and act like we never met. Or we can get him to meet up with us and we can let him know that we know the deal together. Because no matter what you choose to do, the next time I see his ass I'm letting him know that I'm not the one." Angie was in the full facade.

'Let me do some snooping into your story before I take it to the next level. But if this turd smells like shit, then expect a call from me soon." Pulling back up to Angie's car. "Let me ask you one more question before you go. What do you know about Dan?" Gripping her purse.

"You mean his best friend?" Sounding unsure.

"Yeah, his best friend."

"I actually never met him. I've seen pictures of him though. In Mitch's phone. He'd always tease me about him and say that he was his killer. And if he found out that I was cheating on him, then he would send Dan to meet me." Improvising. "I mean I'd say something like. I was going to meet a guy who wants to spend all his time with me. And he'd be like… You're gonna meet Dan. I always just thought he was joking." Seeing her story was working by the tears running down Debbie's cheeks.

"I ain't going to lie. That was a huge pill to swallow, but for what it's worth. Thank you for approaching me like a woman and letting me know what's going on."

"That's all I was trying to do girl. And sorry for bombarding you with all of this out of the blue. I just didn't know how else to approach the situation. Oh, and thank you for not trying to set me up. You can't trust females these days."

"You can't trust nobody these days." Corrected Debbie. Getting her phone out as she pulled off, dialing Mitch's number. "Baby. I got a question for you." Pausing to take a breath. "Ain't Dan's number 330-5267?"

"That's Dan's old number. He got that phone shut off because he lost it when the police were chasing us. Remember cause that's the same time I switched phones." Mitch's voice came through the speakerphone. "What are you asking me about Dan's old number for anyway?"

"The coincidences are unreal. You sure he didn't shut it off because his bitch Angie was pregnant?" Scoffs.

"His bitch who?" Snapping. "Look, I don't have a clue what the fuck you're talking about. I never heard of Angie or a pregnant bitch. The only chick I ever thought he got pregnant was Darla, and he swears that ain't his baby." Frustrated. "I got just a few more errands to run and after that we can sit down and talk so you can tell me what the hell is going on."

"Or so you can try and think of a way to cover up what's going on. Okay, I'll play your game." Speaking calm and soft. "Call me when you get time baby."

"I don't know what you got going on in that little head of yours, but whatever it is, put it on chill until we talk please? You are clearly pissed off about something, and you're purposely diverting what it is, so there's no way I can be on what you're on." Trying to sound soothing. "Listen, just go home and relax. When I get there just give it to me straight, and I'm sure we can get to the bottom of this."

"So, what time do you think you're gonna be home later?"

"You're already mad enough as it is, so I ain't even going to start to guess how long I'm going to be, because I'd be lying to you and you're just going to be even more pisseder."

"Wait." Comprehending. "Did you just say pisseder? Boy, that's not even a word."

"Just like whatever you're mad about probably ain't even a thing."

“I really hate you sometimes.” Sarcastically.

“And I really love you more during those times. Somebody’s gotta be the glue.” Looking out his window. “Look babe, Rodney just came out of the store and he’s about to get in the car. I don’t wanna be talking like this in front of him. I promise I’m going to try and get done as soon as possible so we can talk.” Pausing briefly. “Baby. I love you.”

“I love you too.” Hanging up. “Girl you’re about to lose your shit. Somebody’s lying, and I’m going to find out who. And when I do.” Squeezing the steering wheel. “Oh, shits about to get drastic!”

CHAPTER 12

Leaning on the railing of the patio. “Man, this weed I got from RayRay is on some next-level exotic shit.” Freddie exhales his smoke as he examines his blunt. “Did I mention that this blunt is rolled to perfection?” Holding it up for Paul to see. “You wish you could roll like this.”

“Boy, slow down. I taught you how to roll.”

“So, you’re saying that I don’t roll better than you?”

“I’m saying, I taught you how to roll. I really don't give a fuck who rolls better, as long as the blunt smokes good.”

“That sounds a lot like the saying…” Holding up his quotes. “It don’t matter if you win or lose. And do you know who says that line? The loser!” Pointing at Paul. “You hate to admit that I’m better than you. I bet your girl would say it.”

“That’s because y’all two fuck asses be hating.” Hocking a loogie off the patio. “She knows what it really is though.”

“Yeah, she knows that she really likes to smoke when I roll.”

Squinting to see into a car that was slowing down. “Yo cuz, you see that car right there?” Paul said, pointing with his eyes and a head gesture.

“Yeah, I’m on it.” Freddie says reaching in his back to grip his gun. “I just got this new toy this morning and I’m already going to get to use it. Today must be my lucky day.”

“Nah, don’t dirty your baby. I got something for their ass.” Paul slides his hand under the couch he’d been sitting on and pulls out a TEC-9. Concealing it behind his back. “Let them make one dumb move and it’s going down.”

Astonished by the weaponry Paul has exhibited. “I thought you said you didn’t have nothing.”

“You said you needed something to tote. I got this. The AR-15, and the Mossberg pump. Now that’s sawed off, but I still wouldn’t call it totable. Everything I got is for shit like this. I’m done playing with this dude.”

“Hold on. Hold on. I think I know that car.” Bending over to try and see through the window. “Yurp!” Freddie yells out.

"Y'all look nervous as a bitch up there." Jack's voice came from the car as the tinted window rolled down.

"Nervous my ass!" Paul yelled back, revealing his murder toy.

"You know we ain't never scared!" Freddie followed up by flashing his brand new Beretta 45.

Standing up from the car. "Damn! That's how y'all giving it up?" Holding his hands up. "You know I'm a sucker for gunplay." Pointing back at his car with two females holding up AK-47's.

"They fine as fuck and they shooters. I swear I'ma be just like you when I grow up." Freddie embraced Jack when he walked up.

"If you wanna be like me, then you need to make sure the motherfuckers you kill are dead."

Paul daps him up. "What the fuck you hear out here?"

"It ain't about what I heard. It's about what I know."

"What's that?" Asked Freddie.

"I know that you tried to body Dan yesterday and you only gave him an arm wound."

In disbelief. "You crazy as hell. I shot up that nigga's whole torso!"

"Negative!" Objected Jack. "You shot up that nigga's whole vest. He said the impact knocked him out. When he woke up, you were gone, and he drove off. Unless he's a ghost. I just talked to him like twenty minutes ago. He's driving a black SUV." Shaking his head. "You already know what type of time he's on when you see him. That boy gunning for your head."

"We aint worried about him." Kissing the barrel of his gun. "Aye cuzzo." Getting Paul's attention. "Since that nigga still walking around here, then that means there ain't no bodies on my other gun. I'm going to need you to dig that up for me when you get a chance."

"Shit, I'll go and get that now. Better be safe than sorry." Walking off.

Wiping his sweat with a towel he had draped on his shoulder. "That's y'alls problem right there. Y'all always thinking y'all safe. These streets love nobody. I don't give a fuck if you got a whole squad and a tank around you. You ain't never safe, cause, in all actuality, it's always gonna be a hating ass nigga around your circle that wants to be you."

"I feel you big cuz."

"You say you feel me, but do you? Cause if I gotta tell my big cousins, which happens to be y'alls moms, that something happened to y'all. They ain't gonna let me rest until I kill this whole city. So please be careful, because I got a lot going on and I don't have time to be going to war because you're out here being messy." Faking a two-piece combo at Freddie's chest. "And I'm coming at you because it's always your name I keep hearing in shit. I only hear Paul's name when he's out here helping you clean up your messes."

"You make it seem like I just be out here fucking up. Shit happens out here. I can't stop that." Defensive.

"What you can do, is control what happens around you. If an environment is out of your control, then clearly, it ain't your environment. Move around before you let someone else control your outcome. If shit keeps happening, it's only two things you can change. Where you're at and who you're with." Signaling to his car. "When you're with the right people in the right places, your only outcome should be income. When you get that, then you get me. Until then you're just out here living frivolously with no direction. I know it looks like I do what I want, but actually, I've disciplined myself to do what I needed until it became a habit. Now all I want to do is what I need. Does that make sense to you?"

"I think so. You're basically saying the cool life I see of fun, money, and bad bitches is really an illusion to hide your discipline and focus."

"Not quite, but close enough I guess." After a few seconds of laughter. "You're gonna be alright little cuz." Pulling a wad of money out of his pocket. "I know you got something good to smoke on."

"You know right. I got some sour. And not that fake sour with the seeds that are going around. I got that official sour." Pulling a bag out of his shorts full of ready-bagged weed. "I got quads and eighths."

"Shit." Rubbing his chin, trying to decide. "Let me get three quads."

“You don’t want to open a bag and look at it first?”

“For what? I can see its lime green from here, and I could smell it before you pulled it out. Plus, you and Paul’s eyes are redder than the devil's dick with a heat rash.” Counting out some money. “Two hundred?”

“I’ll do two hundred for you but for anyone else that would be two-fifty all day.”

Peeling off more money. “Well make it three-fifty”

Taking the money. “I said you was good cuz. I wasn’t about to tax you. You’re family.”

“The last jewel I’m going to give you before I roll up out of here. You ready?”

“Always.”

“So, there are three types of people you're gonna attract around you the more money you get. First, you got the ones that want what you got and they’re waiting for the right moment to take over for you or take what you got from you. Find these motherfuckers as soon as possible and get rid of them. I don’t care what they bring to the table. Because they’re setting the tables for themselves, not you. Next, you got those people who love you doing good, because they like the benefits that trickle down to them. Be careful what you let them know about you. Because in the long run you never know if and when they’ll switch sides to your enemy because they’re doing better than you at any moment. Last and definitely not least, you got those people who are around because they really want to see you succeed. You can usually count them on one hand and still have a few fingers left over. So, with that being said. You know who I am.” Grabbing Freddie’s hand and pulling him close to give him a one-arm hug. “You know my number if you need me. I love you boy.” Getting in his car. “Tell Paul I’m going to slide through this weekend, and I want him to light the grill up.”

“I've been trying to get him to get on it, but he’s been bullshitting.”

“I haven’t been bullshitting. It’s just been too hot out here to be standing over a grill all day.” Paul says as he comes through the screen door.

“Well, I got fifty for you if you feel like it next Saturday. And I’ll buy everything you need to cook.”

"Sounds like I'm on the grill next Saturday. Come through early so I can have the meat ready on time."

"I'm going to come on Friday, so you can clean and season it the night before if you want to."

"That'll be perfect."

After Jack pulls off a Lexus pulls up. "I bet this is the shorty that hit me earlier. She said she's Cherry's cousin. I know she sounded fine like Cherry over the phone." Walking up on the car to see a beautiful smile.

"I'm sorry. I'm looking for Freddie. He told me to meet him here."

"I'm Freddie. And you must be Passion." Reaching his hand in her window to shake her hand. "You look even better in person than you sounded on the phone."

"Aww, thanks. You're about to have me out here blushing."

"It's the truth. But what did you say you was trying to get?"

"I just wanted like an eighth or a quarter. Depending on how much."

"Well, my eighths are going for fifty and my quarters a hundred. But for you, give me forty or eighty."

"I'll take the quarter so it can last me a couple of days, but can I ask you a huge favor?"

"Baby, you can ask me anything you want." Giving her a flirty eye.

"Can you roll a couple of blunts for me? I can't roll for shit." Holding up her freshly manicured nails.

"It's funny you say that because I happen to be able to roll my ass off. Ain't that right Paul?"

"You're okay." Paul said nonchalantly.

"And you're a fucking hater!" Leaning down in her window. "I don't mind rolling for you if you let me smoke with you."

"Get in." Passion grabs her shoes from the floor in the front and throws them in the back seat. "I'm sorry, but I don't think your friend can fit back there."

"He's good. Just hang on to that piece for me till I get back." Holding up a gun sign with his fingers.

"I got you but are you sure you don't want to take it just in case."

"What do you think? Do I need that gun?" Freddie questions Passion.

"I don't see why you would need it. I ain't going to try and hurt you. We're just about to go to my hotel room and chill and smoke then I'm going to bring you back here."

"You heard the lady, I'm good. Besides, don't nobody want no smoke with me right now." Freddie hopped in the car, smiling from ear to ear.

Paul watched as they drove off. "That lucky motherfucker."

CHAPTER 13

"Yo!" Dan yells in the house as he lets himself in.

"I didn't hear anyone give you permission to be walking in my house." Snapped Darla as she came towards Dan clutching a big knife.

"Damn baby. What happened to a smile and a hug?" Lifting his shirt to show his piece. "You're really gonna bring a knife to a gunfight?"

"This knife ain't even for you. I was in the kitchen cutting up some roast." Walking back towards the kitchen. "Trust and believe. I got something for your ass." Turning to point her knife at him. "I'm already mad at your ass Dan. I don't even know why I keep on being here for you when you need me."

"Because you love me." Smiling big.

"You don't give a fuck about me, so all that fake lovey-dovey shit don't even matter." Turning to the counter to continue cutting her meat.

"Here you go with this bullshit. I ain't been here for a whole five minutes and you're already tripping." Holding his one good arm in the air. "I come in peace. Damn!" Looking around. "Little niggas in the streets trying to kill me. You want me dead. Who the fuck else I got beef with this week?"

"Don't try and play the victim now. I don't even feel sorry for your ass after all the shit you've said about me."

"I keep telling you, don't stud that shit. I be going overboard on the disrespect to keep you and my son safe. I don't really mean that shit. But you know the type of time I be on out here. A nigga would love to know he could get to me by getting to you."

"Boy, miss me with that bullshit! I talked to Debbie, and she even said that you were talking about me like I'm the scum of the earth. Calling me ugly and shit." Sincerely hurt. "Mitch is supposed to be the fam and you can't even keep it real with him?"

"Who do you think got me shot? Hell nah, I can't let him know that you and little man mean the world to me!" Bringing his voice down. "The day I always told you about, when our secrecy was really gonna matter, is today. I always told you actions speak louder than words, didn't I?"

"Yeah."

"Then what do my actions say? When was the last time you paid your own rent or bills?" Putting his hand to his ear.

"The month I told you I was pregnant?"

"So don't let what I say to motherfuckers that don't mean shit to me, get to you. I tell a motherfucker what I want him to know. I show you what's real." Pulling Darla towards him by her shirt. "Now what's up? You gonna get me right or what?"

Poking his hand with the tip of the knife. "Get your hands off me! I got your back, but we ain't that cool yet."

"Bitch!" Dan balled up his fist and held it up to her face.

"Punch me if you want to and see how many holes you leave here with."

Taking a step back. "Your ass is crazy!" Letting off a grin. "I ain't even about to fuck with you like that."

"So, you really expect me to believe that the main person you're with every day. Your ace boon coon. Your best friend. Hell, you're brother." Staring him firm in the eyes, still gripping the knife. "Is the one that got you shot?" Shaking her head. "What the fuck did you go and do now?"

"Damn! Why I had to do something?" Shrugging his shoulders. "Why couldn't it be him that got this shit started?"

"Was it?" Still locking eyes.

"Stop giving me that look. I ain't gonna lie to you. He's been trying to block me out from the plug, so I tried to get rid of him. You know my motto, if you're in my way then I'm going to send you on your way. And some things are just bigger than friendship. I ain't about to let nobody starve me or even control how much I eat."

"By the looks of your arm in a sling, that didn't go so well for you. Maybe you should've gone a different route. Like, maybe try to talk to him. I don't know." Juggling her hands. "Let him know where you stand."

"What the fuck I look like pleading my case to another man about my placement in these streets. I take what I want and that's how it's gonna be."

"You're so fucked up." Insulted Darla.

"Nobody ever gained an empire by asking for it. Shit, even America got taken from the Indians and the Indigenous Blacks. I'm just living the American way." Taking a piece of the roast and tossing it in his mouth. "Oh, that's good."

"I'll make you a plate when I'm done with your arm." Sliding a chair from under the table. "Sit here so I can use this bright light." Turning the knob on the wall to brighten the chandelier. "I'll be right back. I gotta go grab my kit out of my room."

Watching her walk away. "Do you need some help finding it back there? I could help you if you'd like." Flirty.

"I thought I was so ugly."

"You are. But your ass is so beautiful." Seeing Darla disappear into her bedroom, Dan puts a wad of cash in a coffee can, in her cabinet. "You need to let me go ahead and pay to get your teeth fixed, and then I wouldn't have anything to say." Sitting back down. "Shit. How long do you think it's going to take you to fill up your little can in the cabinet? You just need to let me give you a one-time personal loan. Interest-free. Except for my interest. And I'm sure we can work out a way you can pay me back, so you don't gotta feel so guilty about me doing it for you."

Coming back from the room holding her medical bag. "You already do enough keeping me in this neighborhood so your son can go to a good school when it comes time. You don't know how thankful I am that he doesn't gotta see crackheads on the corner every day when he goes outside to play. I don't need you fixing me. Just take care of your son. I'm not your woman, remember? Besides, my can will be ready faster than you know it." Setting her supplies up on the table. "Anyways, you don't be complaining when I'm sucking your dick. Don't nothing be wrong with my teeth then."

"I agree. There's nothing wrong with the first thirty-two of them. But then their other eight siblings go cramming themselves in there somehow. And don't lie. You used to be scrappy Becky until you learned how to control them motherfuckers."

Flicking him off. "Fuck you. You're such an asshole."

"Nah, but for real, if you fix that grill and pull your hairline down some over your forehead, you'd be finer than a bitch." laughing.

“I hate you!” Shoving his head. “So, what are you going to do about Mitch? You can’t just sit around and wait for him to kill you.” Helping Dan pull his shirt over his head.

“You know I ain’t goin out like that. I got a little something planned for his ass.” Rubbing her butt. “You sound like you're down with a one eighty-seven.”

“I ain’t about to let someone kill you before I get to. You’re the only baby daddy I got. Even though I can’t stand you sometimes.” Propping a towel under his arm. “This is just saline I’m using to clean it with. Do this at least four times a day for the first couple of weeks. Make sure you do, so you don’t run the risk of infection.”

“So basically, do all the same shit you had me doing when I got shot in the leg?”

“Pretty much. It’s just another bullet hole.” Securing her wrap with tape. “One of these days you’re gonna get yourself shot and I’m not going to be able to fix it.”

Knocking on the table. “You better knock on wood too, after saying that shit. Don’t be trying to jinx me out here. Words are powerful.” Watching her wrap his wounds with precision. “All I need you to do is stay out the way and take care of little man. I got another bitch to shoot for me.” Wincing. “Damn! Do you think you did it tight enough?”

“Don’t stop being a tough guy now.” Helping him put his shirt back on. “You’re going to need to keep that same energy if you want to win this war. You know how Mitch is.”

“Just like I know how I am. I got this.” Rising from the table. “Thanks for getting me right.” Looking at his arm in the mirror. “My baby momma the nurse.” Smiling at Darla. “So, what you got going on, for real?”

“What are you talking about?” Giving him a coy smile.

Stepping into her space. “Don’t act stupid with me. I told you I was coming over. You got rid of my son.”

“He’s over my mother’s, so I can go to work.” Turning to look in the refrigerator and fanning herself. “It’s hot in here. Do you want something to drink?”

Grabbing Darla’s arm and turning her back around to face him. “Stop playing with me. You don’t go to work until tomorrow. So, as I said… you got rid of my son. You're wearing these tiny ass boxer shorts, letting all your cake hang out." Smacking her butt. "Just say you want me to stay the night so we can play house."

"We played house three years ago, and my baby daddy still hasn't come back home from work."

Pecking her neck. "I see you got jokes." Whispering in her ear. "Why did you make my favorite meal if you didn't want me to stay?"

Leaning her head to the side and exhaling deeply. "Since when was roast your favorite meal?"

Rubbing her clit through her shorts. "I wasn't talking about the roast."

CHAPTER 14

"So let me get this straight." Rodney checks his headlights to ensure they are on. "Elijah has been down here for a minute now, and he's your closest cousin and Dan has been your best friend since you were in elementary school. Yet, neither one of them has ever met each other?"

"Correct" Confirms Mitch.

"Talk about living a double life."

"We all live double lives at one point in our lives. Whether it's not letting your mom know you smoke weed or trying to make a girl believe your something you're not. Some of us are just more aware of the fact."

Smirking. "And see, everything makes sense. I'm like why is he the only person that always talks smart. Who the hell do you talk to when nobody's around? Then I met Elijah."

"Yeah, his mom used to make me read so many books over the summer. And she used to be a stickler for grammar."

"See, that's what I'm talking about. Who the fuck says stickler?" Laughing.

"A lot of people. You just need to get some better friends."

"One thing about friends with extensive vocabularies, is they stay long-winded. Ya, feel me? I like my friends silent and short-spoken." Voiced Rodney.

"I can't knock you for that. All I'ma say to you is… If you're flying with the pigeons, you'll never understand the freedom to fly like an eagle."

"What the fuck is that supposed to mean? You know I ain't good with all those philosophical quotes you be spitting."

"It means, fuck with me. I'm a motherfucking eagle. Your homeboys you be with on the block, they're pigeons. I hunt my prey down, so I eat my food fresh. They eat scraps of food that get thrown to them by people. I navigate alone. They move in flocks."

"So, what am I?" Asked Rodney.

"Depends on who you're with." Grinning. "Hey, slow down." Pointing at the store parking lot. "Ain't that Dan's car right there?" Taking his gun off safety. "Go, back in, across the street, and kill the lights. I'm going to go stand over there on the side of the building. When you see him come out, give me the sign, and I'm going to pop out and take his head off." Hopping out of the car. "Then it's game over."

"Aye aye captain." Rodney backed the car in the driveway, as he was instructed and watched the store anxiously. "C'mon bitch! Get your stupid ass out the way before you get shot." Seeing an old lady come out of the store and bending down to tie her shoes."

After hearing the sound of the door open and close, Mitch starts running down times in his head that he was there for Dan. "After all we've been through. This is how we gotta be. Fuck it!" Talking to himself to motivate his rage. "Ain't no coming back from this now." Seeing Rodney signal by slicing his throat. Pistol up and ready to blow, he makes a stealthy dart around the corner and runs up, hand tensing, ready to pull the trigger. "What the fuck?"

"Yo my man. You can have everything I got! Please don't shoot me." The middle-aged man cried out.

Realizing it was the wrong person, Mitch tucked his gun and ran across the street, and jumped back in the car. "Go! Go! Go!" After they sped off, "Bro! You had me about to shoot the wrong person. Good thing I aim first and don't just shoot with my eyes closed."

"You're trippin. I was telling you to abort, abort." Repeating the same hand signal as before.

"I thought you was saying take his head off." Imitating his gesture. "Boy, I was about to give my buddy the business." They both begin laughing. "But on a serious note, we're gonna have to work on our hand signals. You never know when we're gonna need to be on the same page again."

"Agreed." Getting back on task. "Speaking of being on the same page. We still need to holla at Freddie and let him know his job is incomplete."

"Shit, pull up. You know they're probably sitting out on the porch. Booming the weed."

"Hell yeah. I need me a sack of that shit they had the other day. Boy, I was high as a giraffe ass."

"You ain't lying. If you weren't my man, one hundred grand, I might've thought you were smoking on something else the way you were moving all slow and paranoid."

"I didn't tell you?"

"Tell me what?"

Taking a pause not to laugh, "You remember before I picked you up, I was at old girls house with all the kids?"

"Right. I remember that's where you said you were at. Because I said she looked like a duck with her chicks, walking to the store."

"So, before I left, I saw a plate of cookies on the table and I grabbed a few, and them bitches was good as fuck. Well to make a long story longer. She made them with THC, so I was way out of my element."

"So, she just watched you eat all those cookies, and didn't say nothing?" Shaking his head. "Man, that's fucked up."

"She gonna tell me after I ate my fifth one to slow down cause they were special cookies." Thinking back. "I should've known something was up, just by the way she was smiling while she watched me eat them." Looking ahead to Paul's house. "You was right again." Pointing at Paul making a sale. "That boy is out here getting it. I don't see Freddie though."

"What's up?" Paul raises his hands and speaks when he notices it's Mitch in the car. "I didn't know that was you for a second. You're always in something else when I see you."

Getting out of the car, "You know I gotta switch it up just in case the feds are watching."

"I know that's right. I'm trying to stay low my damn self." Confirmed Paul.

"Where is Freddie's crazy ass at?"

"Ain't no telling where that boy is. All I know is he sold some bad light-skinned chick a bag and they left to go smoke. I don't know what it is about that little baby face motherfucker, but the bitches love his ass." Laughing at his own thoughts. "I be feeling like I'm his backup dancer when we be having bitches over."

"Sounds like you're a little jealous." Teased Rodney.

"Never that. I be happy to see that little cuz got the juice. It ain't like I don't pull bitches. It just seems like I be having to work harder than his Rico Suave lookin ass."

"We came over to tell him to be watchful. I had him do a little something for me, and that shit didn't go according to plan."

"What? You talking about that shit with Dan?"

"Yeah. I wasn't sure if he told you or not. I didn't want to blow his cover."

"He knows Dan's not dead. Our cousin Jack came over here earlier and told him."

"Jack's ass always knows something." Says Mitch.

"I don't know what pipeline he gets his information from, but he is always on point," Rodney added.

"You're right because I still don't know how he knew about that shit we did in Youngstown." Tapping Rodney's arm. "I was almost certain you were playing both sides for a minute."

"Hell nah! I never went against the team. I didn't ever say anything to anybody about anything. Ya feel me?" convinces Rodney.

"G's up." Paul gives Rodney dap. "Snitching is so overrated out here these days. I remember when I was coming up gossiping was considered a form of snitching. Now everybody tells everybody's business."

"Or this new shit of recording and posting everything like the feds don't use social media."

"You can't forget where they get it from." Mitch commented. "All these rappers, self-snitching. They put everything in a song except for their social security number. Then wonder how they catch cases. This shit is crazy."

"This is Freddie right here." Paul begins reading an incoming text aloud. "He says, don't wait up for me. I think she's feeling the kid." Texting back. "You dirty little whore."

"Now that we know that he's straight. What's up with a bag? I hope you got some more of that good shit you had last time." Rodney suggested.

"That shit went so fast, but for real, I think the batch I got now is even better." Sparking up a blunt. "Taste this. Let me know if you're fucking with it." Handing it to Rodney.

Coughing repeatedly. "Fuck! That went straight to my lungs. Let me get a quarter."

“After you get that we gotta run. I got a couple more stops to make before I get up with Debbie. I still don’t know what she was talking about earlier. All I know is she was trippin.”

CHAPTER 15

Passion pulls up in front of her room. “Don’t think we’re fucking because I got you at a hotel. I just don’t like to drive and smoke. It makes me feel paranoid.”

“Damn baby girl, do I give you the vibe of a pervert or something?” On the defensive. “Let’s make a deal.” Reaching his hand out to make a pact. “I promise not to touch you as long as you promise to keep your hands off my sexy physique,” Freddie said, rubbing his defined chest. “So, you shook on it. Don’t get me in here and try to take advantage of me.” Trying to sound like a little girl.

“You’re funny.” Getting her key card out of her pocketbook. “I just gotta be upfront because dudes are thirsty as hell. You can’t even tell a guy you like his shoes, without him thinking he can fuck.”

Freddie sat down at the table and started to roll immediately. “You act like females are a whole lot different.” Argumentative. “Boom, a dude probably don’t even want to holler. A broad will have the brightest color hair and nails long as a bitch to match. Sexy ass dress on.” Describing Passion’s appearance. “And somebody like myself could notice and be like Damn ma, your style is all that. And she’ll say some shit like, don’t think we fucking because you like my dress.” Laughing. “I’m just saying. You can’t even pass a compliment without it going to a female's head.”

Looking disgusted. “That was mean. I don’t think I like you no more.” Trying not to break a smile.

“Well, that makes both of us. So, you don’t got nothing to worry about except for smoking some good weed.” Putting fire to his blunt. “Now I’m a very forgiving person, so halfway through the blunt, I might start to like you again.”

“You’re lucky you’re kinda cute, or I’d be offended.” Assures Passion.

“I don’t mean no harm. I just like to have fun.”

“So, when we were in the car and I asked you why you had your seat all the way back, you said something about somebody might want to shoot you back." Changing direction. "I can't even imagine you involved in anything violent. You just have such a babyface."

Gripping his chin. "I don't know if that's a compliment or not, but I don't just be violent all the time. But this city is crazy. They prey on the weak."

"So, what did you have to shoot somebody for?"

Looking at her with a serious look. "I really don't do too much pillow talking about street shit but being that you don't know anybody I'm about to talk about. What the hell." Breaking down more weed on the table for his next blunt. "So, it's one dude who we're just gonna call snitch for the story. And he had a friend named truth. One day snitch got himself in some kind of trouble with the law and he made a deal that he would set up some people to get arrested if the police left him alone. But from how I got it, he was a big fish giving up minnows and the police wasn't satisfied, so they told him to give them someone bigger or he was going to renege on their deal."

Interrupting his story. "So, I take it you got your version of the story from Truth?"

"Nah, I got my version of the story from Inmate. One of the first minnows to go down. And I just been paying attention to the streets, watching how shit's been going down." Recollecting his thoughts. "So, it was said that Truth had the best plug, and Snitch wanted it, so he set him up. Only he knew that unlike the other people he set up. If Truth went to jail, he had enough money to get back out, and it was a possibility of him finding out that he set him up in the first place. So, he told the officer to kill Truth. Take half the dope and all the credit for a hell of a sizable drug bust where the suspect pulled a gun and had to be shot. Only before their plan could happen, Truth got away."

"Damn. That shit sounds crazy. So, are you Truth?" Pretending to be shocked at what she was hearing.

Letting out a giggle. "Nah. But I was cool with both of them. So, truth offered me some money to take out Snitch and I accepted. Only when I went to do the job, Snitch offered me way less money to kill Truth." Seeing her confused face. "Am I losing you?"

“No. I’m just thinking to myself. What are the odds that both of them would try to hire you? Are you some sort of hitman or something?”

“Now that’s a whole other story altogether. Let’s get through this one first.”

“Okay”

“Now where was I? Oh yeah, So boom. I told him I was accepting his offer and he gave me half of the bread up front, and I shot him.” Come to find out, he was wearing a vest so he’s still alive.”

“Aren’t you scared that he’s going to kill you, or get you killed? You said he’s a big fish.”

“I ain’t never died before to be scared of it. When my time is up, my clock will stop. Until that time. Tick tock, tick tock.” Moving his finger with each tick.

“Maybe you should’ve taken that gun from your cousin.”

“I’m good. I got you to protect me.” Passing a wink, and a smile.

“Hearing a knock at the door. “That’s probably my cousin. I told her to swing by and smoke with me. I wasn’t expecting that I was going to be having you over. I’m sorry.”

“You’re good.” Freddie went back to rolling his next blunt.

“Yeah, bitch nigga!” Dan barged in the room with his gun drawn at Freddie.

Standing to his feet, dropping the blunt in his hand. “Bitch, you set me up!”

“You thought you was going to get away with shooting me motherfucker!” Poking the barrel of his gun into Freddie’s forehead. “Sit your ass down.

“Dan, don’t shoot him!” Passion pleaded.

“What the fuck you mean don’t shoot him? Bitch have you lost your mind?” Pointing his gun at her then back at him. “I just want to know why you double-crossed me before I noodle your ass.”

“Nigga, you double-crossed the whole hood. Like nobody knows it's you setting everybody up. If you’re gonna shoot me, get to it!” Gritting his teeth.

Dan Smirking. “So, you think you know something?”

“I know that you're a snitch.”

"Open up." Forcing his barrel into Freddie's mouth. "Who the fuck you calling a snitch?"

Passion grabbed Dan's arm and tried to pull him back. "Stop!"

"Bitch, you're going to make me kill both of y'all in this motherfucker." Turning to push her across the room. "Now back the fuck up!" Turning back to point his gun at Freddie.

"Put your gun down!" Passion grabbed her gun out of her purse on the bed and put it to the back of Dan's head. "I'm not playing with you! Put it down."

As soon as Dan's gun hit the table, Freddie pulled the gun from his waist, which he had concealed the whole time. "I guess it ain't my time." Pointing his gun at Passion who had her gun pointed back at him. "And I was almost about to forgive you."

Seeing Freddie go out the door, Dan picks his gun up and chases behind him. "Pussy!" Letting off a shot, seeing that he wasn't going to catch him. "I'm going to kill the fuck out of this kid." Returning to the room. "What the fuck was that about?" Walking up on her in rage.

Backing up. "I didn't want you to shoot him yet. I need him to get me close to Mitch. That's the real target ain't it?"

Raising his hand to threaten her. "Bitch don't fucking play with me. You better start saying something that makes sense."

"So, I went and met with Debbie as you asked, and she questioned me about you. Mitch pretty much pushed me away because of you. Now that I stopped you from killing Freddie. I know that he's going to tell Mitch. So, when I tell her my sob story about how I didn't know what you were on and when I found out I turned on you, she might just trust me."

"So why did you lie to me and say that he didn't have a gun?"

"He lied to me. I swear I didn't know."

Calmly. "I just wish you would've told me cause I would've carried it way different. I would've probably just blown his shit out the gate." Stroking her hair. "You think I'm some type of sucker or something?" Snatching her by her hair and throwing her to the bed before putting his gun to her head. "I swear if I didn't need your pretty little face so bad to pull this off, I'd beat your fucking nose in right now with the butt of my gun. If you ever pull a gun on me again." Punching her in the stomach and walking away. "Get your shit. We gotta get out of here."

After rolling side to side in pain, Passion gets herself together and begins to smile in anger.

CHAPTER 16

"Fancy seeing you around here." Elijah leans forward and looks both ways up his street before backing his wheelchair out of the doorway to let Debbie in.

"I'm sorry to barge in on you like this Elijah, but I really need to talk to you. And I didn't want to have this conversation over the phone."

Locking all the locks on his door. "No need to be sorry. We're family. My door is always open to you." Gliding by. "Come back here. This seems like it's going to take a while."

Walking past the kitchen. "You just had someone mop your floor?"

"Yeah." Letting out a giggle. "I had me mop my floor. I was just about to set the fan up so it could dry fast when my motion detector let me know you were pulling up." Looking down at his legs. "That's why my pants are all wet. I was all over that floor."

"I told you before. I don't mind coming over to help out if you need me to."

"And I told you, my legs may not work but I'm not an invalent. I can still do what I gotta do to take care of myself." Pointing at the table in the corner. "You can make yourself a drink. I got some of what you like over there, and a couple of different juices in the mini-fridge to mix it with."

"I ain't even going to lie. I really do need a drink right now. I have been having the craziest day today." Measuring out her portions. "First of all, I get a text from some random bitch named Angie, telling me she's fucking with Mitch." Tasting her potion. "So, you know me. I'm like if this groupie don't get off my line. But then she sends me a receipt text. Showing me Mitch's number telling her to meet him at the hotel."

"Are you serious?"

"You see the tears in my eyes. You're fucking right I'm serious. And I am so mad, I can feel my blood boiling." Making two tight fists. "So, I go and meet up with her and she's telling me all kinds of shit that only somebody that really fucks with Mitch would know."

“What did she look like?”

“That’s the crazy part. The little bitch looked good as hell. I can hardly blame him for being attracted to her. But having a whole relationship?”

Shaking his head. “And where did she say she met him at?”

“She said they met at a concert in Virginia. And that she and her cousin had a threesome with him that night after the concert on some wild shit. But they kept linking up ever since then.” Chugging down a shot of her drink. “This bitch even knew he can’t have kids and why.”

“Damn! She knew all the business.” Pecking away at his computer. “Is this her?” Pulling up Passion’s picture.

“How the fuck did you know who I was talking about.” Shaking in anger. “So, this bitch was telling the whole truth so help her God.”

“No, not quite. Just calm down and listen.”

“I’m listening. Now, how did you know it was her?”

“I knew because I don’t believe in coincidence. This same female in this pic tried to set Mitch up the other day. He met her in the mall. But look at this pic, does that hat look familiar to you in the back window?”

“I’ll be damned! Is that one of the hats to those outfits they had made? So that’s Dan’s girl?” Putting her hands on her head. “Now it all makes sense. That’s how she knew so much. And to think, I was about to lay into his ass later.” Laughing at herself. “I’m glad I came to talk to you first.”

“Did she say where she’s staying?”

“No. She just mentioned she was staying at a hotel. But she did say that she wanted to meet up with Mitch together to confront him.” Thinking back. “And I even asked her if she knew Dan because shit just didn’t feel right to me. And you know how I am about my intuition feelings. I couldn’t rest until I made sense of all this.” Going back to refill her glass. “I’m sorry for drinking all your liquor. I’ll buy you another bottle.”

“I’m not worried about that bottle. You know I don't really drink. If you notice, I bought a bottle of everybody's favorite drink. So technically, that was your bottle in the first place.”

“You act like you knew I was coming over.”

"I knew you would one day. And look at you." Motioning his hand like a magician revealing something. "Wa-lah."

"Well, I'm glad you did, because I definitely needed this today." Going back over the bottles. "So, who drinks this one?"

"Oh, that one's Rodney's."

"But it's already been cracked."

"Yeah, because he cracked it."

"Okay, I'm all the way out of the loop now. When did this happen? Because I always know who knows who, so I don't mention the wrong person at the wrong time."

"We just met the other day after all that shit went down with Mitch and that undercover."

"Did you tell him everything?"

"It was the only way to properly introduce myself. But I must say, he was so appreciative after hearing what all I had done."

"I bet he was. But I'm glad y'all finally met. He's a good kid. And he's very loyal to Mitch. But I'm sure you already know that."

"Definitely. But while we're on the subject about being loyal to Mitch, what's your next move with this girl?" Looking intense.

"I don't know. I mean, knowing what I know now. That the whole reason she wanted me to put the little private meeting with Mitch together, was to set him up. I think I'm just going to let Mitch know what happened and go from there. What would you do if you were me?" Looking desperate and confused.

"I think you should set up the meeting." Smiling from ear to ear.

CHAPTER 17

"So where did he say he was going to be?" Mitch turned to ask Paul who was in the back seat.

"He said he ran behind the hotel into the neighborhood. He didn't want to be on the main road and run back into Dan."

"He's not wrong." Agreed Mitch. "I would've done the same thing. Call his phone and tell him where we're at. He should be close by."

Rodney adjusts his rearview mirror to see someone in the street waving their arms. "Don't worry about that call. I think I found him." Slowing down to a halt.

"You good cuz?" Paul asked Freddie, as he got in the car.

"Hell yeah, I'm good. But peep this… Boom, it was the bitch that set me up!"

"Not the fine ass model bitch?" Protested Paul.

"That bitch had me up in here rolling up. She got me thinking her homegirl was coming to smoke with us, so I'm thinking to myself, Boom! If I play my cards right, this might be a possible threesome. Next thing I know this nigga bust in the room and he got the drop on me. I didn't have time to even up my shit."

"So how did you get out of there?" Paul questioned.

"Believe it or not, the bitch pulled out on Dan and made him let me go. I don't know what made her have a change of heart, but I thank God she did. Cause I was a dead man." Shaking his head. "I think I'm still gonna have to kill her ass. I wish I could've fucked first at least."

Paul looked at Freddie sideways. "So, this bitch set you up and you're still thinking about fucking her?"

"Nigga, you have seen how bad she was when she picked me up. Hell yeah, I'm still thinking about fucking her." Laughing at himself.

"Hold on. Was this bitch name Passion?" Asked Mitch.

"Damn, you know my bitch?"

"Obviously better than you. I didn't trust her from the gate." Taunted Mitch.

Pulling into the hotel parking lot. “Where was her room at? In the front or the back?”

“In the back, on the side the dumpster is on.” Pointing at a gap in the trees. “That’s where I ran through to end up in that neighborhood. I thought he was gonna keep chasing me, but he just let off a couple of shots and went back in the room.” Speaking in a whisper. “Oh shit. That’s where her room was.” Pointing to two police cars parked right in front of the door. “I don’t see her car, so they probably bounced.”

Turning the car around. “This is the second time we thought we had this motherfucker tonight!” Rodney spoke in frustration.

“Don’t worry, he can’t hide forever.” Assured Mitch. “Just be patient. We’re gonna run into his ass, and when we do it’s lullabies for him and his little setup bitch!”

Freddie began thinking to himself about how Passion put her gun to Dan’s head in his defense. “I don’t wanna sound like no bitch or nothing, but I feel like we should let the bitch live.”

“Let that bitch live?” Paul's voice screeched. “Nigga, is you crazy?”

“Man, y’all ain’t see how she got me the fuck up out of there. It’s like something happened and she wasn’t down with the shits no more.” At a loss for words. “I can’t really explain it, but I swear I just watched her switch up on him.”

“Well, I agree with Paul.” Joking. “I think you just got too close to the pussy, and you're tryna figure out a way to get back in. The only smart answer to that question is, let her set your dumb ass up again. Maybe next time you can fuck first.” Rodney let out a chuckle.

“That bitch is expired. Time to get her off the shelf. Period!” Mitch added. “And what are we going to do about this unpaid balance between us?” Looking out his rear-view mirror to make sure they weren't being followed.

“You know I ain’t out to get you. I didn’t spend shit yet. I’ma just give it back to you.”

“I got a better idea. Why don’t you just finish the job? This time I’m going to work out all the kinks in the beginning, so we don’t end up back like this. Do you have somewhere you can lay low until I get a location on this motherfucker?”

"I'm good. I'm about to post up at the spot with my back against the wall and my barrel to the world. He can run his ass up on these bullets if he wants to."

Paul gave Freddie dap in agreement. "He's gonna run back up out that bitch in a hearse. I ain't playing no games."

Ceasing their confidence. "Y'all acting a little bit cocky about a situation that can go either way. Just know, that I might be the most calculated person y'all know. But by far, Dan is the most cunning. If you think it's gonna be that easy, like he's just going to walk himself into a hail of bullets on some suicidal dumb shit then you're already losing the battle by underestimating your opponent. One thing I know about Dan is, even when he's being hunted, he's still a hunter." Looking in the backseat to connect eyes with them. "Dan's a fucking shark!"

"So, what are you tryna say? That we're some guppies?" Freddie contested.

"I ain't no motherfucking guppy." Stressed Paul.

"I didn't call y'all guppies. That's what you called yourselves. I was just making a point if you would've let me finish. Which happens to be a scientific fact. A shark can't swim backward, therefore it is physically impossible to back a shark in a corner. So, me calling him a shark ain't about me doubting if you got heart. It's about me knowing the heart of your opposition."

Freddie, trying to speak calmly and not show his inner rage. "I feel where you're coming from and all big dawg, but in all honesty, I ain't trying to back him in a corner. I'm trying to lay his ass in a hearse. The way I see it, we're one and one. We gotta go another round to see who gets the best out of three."

"And that'll be you if you don't put yourself in his world."

"What do you mean?"

"I mean, when I said he was a shark you made yourself a fish. Now him being a shark, he's the toughest in the water. So, you being a fish made you food. What eats sharks?"

Looking over his shoulder at two puzzled faces, Rodney speaks up. "The answer is people, people eat sharks. So, make yourself a fisherman. Now, you're the right type of hunter you need to be to kill a shark."

"Bam!" Mitch reaches his hand out to dap Rodney. "You see that! That's why I fuck with you." Motioning his two fingers back and forth in front of his eyes. "You get me."

"Okay, now I get where you're coming from. But how is that going to help me hunt his bitch ass down?"

"Well first of all you don't hunt sharks down. You put out bait and let them come to you. Trust me. I don't doubt in my mind, that Dan is planning another way to attack us as we speak. That's why I want y'all to lay low until I get a grip on the situation."

"You know I stay low." Paul turned to face Freddie. "It's this little motherfucker you gotta watch out for. He's the one that never sits still."

"Don't nobody gotta watch me. I'm good." Seeing they were approaching Paul's house. "For real, I know it might be a lot, but do you think you could drop me off in Warren Heights? I'm trying to go lay at my bitch house."

Mitch feeling uneasy. "I don't mind taking you wherever you want to go, but do you think it's smart to go chill in the Heights? You know how much motherfuckers love running their mouths about who they see."

"I'm good out there. For one, I'm in the back by the woods. My cousins are gonna be sitting outside all night hustling. If they even think they see that nigga they lighting shit up." Tapping the side of his head. "See, I be paying attention, even when you think I'm not. I know people talk. That's why I picked the Heights. But while he's positioning himself to get me. I already got him."

Rodney looked back at Paul. "It sounds like you need to be rolling with him."

"I'm good. I got my own plan." Pulling out his gun and kissing it before getting out of the car. "Y'all be safe out there. Hit me up in the morning Freddie." Noticing a silver car with rims and tint parked on the side of the road as they pulled off. "Yo, pull up on that car and see who's in it." Cocking his pistol. I ain't never seen that car before in my life."

Mitch took his gun off safety. "Yeah, I was looking at that car when we pulled up."

Paul crept up on one side of the car while Rodney pulled on the other side. "Ain't nobody in it. Must be one of these baby mama's little boyfriends or something."

"You good then?" Rodney waited for Paul's approval.

"Yeah, I'm good." Waving them off and whistling up to his porch. "Man, I gotta piss like a motherfucker!" Fumbling with his keys. "Open the fuck up!" Rushing straight to the toilet, Paul leans his head back and sighs in relief. "Man, that shit was crucial" When Paul steps back into the hallway, he flinches from the sight of a hooded figure coming towards him fast with his gun pointed.

"Where the fuck is Freddie?" Dan ran up on Paul and put his gun in his face. "I didn't come here for you Paul." Poking his gun into his head. "You can live if you choose to, but you're gonna die for sure if you don't tell me something fast!"

"How the fuck you get up in here?"

"Man, you think this is a fucking game.!" Bashing Paul across his forehead with his gun. "I'm asking the fucking questions here, and I see that motherfuckin gun in your pants. If you make any dumb moves, I'm squeezing. Now drop that shit on the fuckin floor before I kill your ass prematurely."

Putting his hands in the air, after tossing his gun away. "I don't know, I swear. He just dropped me off and left with Mitch."

"Where are they going?"

"I don't know! But, if you're gonna shoot me then get on with it. I ain't got all day." Paul said in rage as he wiped the blood from his eyes with his shirt sleeve.

"Don't worry bitch. I'm gonna check you out of here soon enough, but before I do, you're about to call that little wanna be killer back here." Reaching his phone out to Paul.

"I ain't calling shit for you. You know his number."

"You're absolutely right." Dialing Freddie's number, Dan put his phone on speaker.

"What the fuck you doing calling my phone, pussy!"

"You better calm your little bitch ass down and hear what the fuck I got to say."

"I ain't gotta hear shit you gotta say, pussy!"

"Well, maybe you'll listen to what your cousin Paul has to say. Say something bitch." Cracking Paul in the head again with his gun to make him yell out but he only lets out a grunt. "Well, he's acting like he's shy all of a sudden, but check this out."

Pow! Dan shot Paul in the leg and smiled in pleasure as he heard him scream out in agony. "You hear that shit? That's what pussy sounds like!" Yelling on the phone. "Now do I have your motherfuckin attention?" Pow! Pow! Pow! Pow! "You're next bitch!" Dan stood over Paul's twitching body, intrigued by his gurgling and gasping. Smiling as he watched the blood soak his shirt from the holes in his chest as more blood poured out of his mouth. "Don't worry. By this time tomorrow, I'm gonna make sure I send you plenty of company in hell. This shit wouldn't have even had to happen if your cousin would've just kept his nose out of grown folk's business." Bending down to retrieve the gun that Paul had dropped before running out the front door, hopping in his car, and speeding off.

CHAPTER 18

"Shhh! Shhh!" Debbie held her phone up to show Elijah her incoming call. "This is her right here."

"Remember how we planned it." Coached Elijah.

"I'm so drunk. I hope I don't fuck this up." Trying to gain her composure before answering on speakerphone. "Hello."

"Hey Debbie, this is Angie. I know you said that you would call me, but I felt like I needed to call you and keep shit a buck with you."

"You have my attention."

"Well, you know how you asked me if I knew Dan, and I said I never met him before?"

"Of course, I remember."

"The truth is that I do know Dan, and I never met Mitch. That is until the other day in the mall. Dan sent me to get at Mitch before he sent me to get at you. He figured that you would be easier to get to."

"So, what happened when you met Mitch, for real?"

"For real… He told me he was a very busy person, and he didn't have time to get to know me. Then he paid me to leave him alone. I can say that was literally one of the most embarrassing moments in my life. I mean I've set up plenty of dudes before. Never has anyone ever paid me to go away."

Covering her mouth to keep from laughing. "Now that story sounds more like my Mitch. So how long have you known Dan?"

"I've been kickin it with Dan for a minute now. At least five years. And I've done a lot of shystie jobs with him if you know what I mean. And after all these years we have grown closer than ever to the point that I thought we had a real relationship going on. Now, I'm not dumb but I know he still has his little bitches here and there, but I just thought I was the one."

"So what? You're calling me because you found out he's cheating on you?" Debbie interrupted.

"No. I'm calling you because I have learned how much of a bad person he actually is, and how he's got me down here setting up good people over some shady shit he's been doing."

"Like what?"

"Well, first of all, he told me that Mitch was a snitch and that he tried to get him murdered by an undercover. But when I had Mitch's little homeboy Freddie at my room, he gave me a whole other story about how Dan was setting up other dudes from around here with the same undercover." Angie paused and took a deep breath. "Now while he had me getting him close to the dudes he wanted to kill, he let me get too close to the truth, and I'm not about to help him just murder innocent people for this small change."

"Well, I'm going to keep it a buck with you as well. I knew you were sent by Dan the whole time. I just wanted to see if you were going to admit it. But the fact that you lied at first and now you're trying to double back, I don't know if I can trust you."

"I'm telling you the truth. I lied because I was really on his side. I thought Mitch and Freddie were foul. I just saved Freddie from Dan shooting him earlier."

"What!" Debbie in shock.

"Yeah, I had him come smoke with me at the hotel and Dan was supposed to run in and kill him. But like I said, he was so real about everything, I knew he wasn't lying. So, when Dan came in, I pulled out on Dan and gave Freddie a chance to escape. Now I want to help y'all get him before he gets y'all. Just tell me what you need me to do."

"Text me when he gets around and I'm going to call you with a place to meet up with me and Mitch tomorrow. I'm going to make it seem like I'm so hurt that Mitch is cheating on me, and I'm going to thank you as a woman for keeping it real with me. He's so arrogant that he's gonna believe y'alls plan is working. Next, you get him to the location I give you and I'll handle it from there." A brief silence. "Oh yeah, one more thing."

"What's that?"

"If I feel you're trying to deceive me again in any way, I promise on my life, I'm going to kill you in the worst way."

"You'll see how genuine I'm being with you. But after I hold up my end, can I trust you not to let your boyfriend and his friends kill me."

"Girl, if you help us get Dan, not only will I assure you won't get harmed, but I will personally make sure that you're compensated well for your assistance."

"Okay. I don't know what he's out doing but he's got me waiting on him to get me somewhere to stay the night since I can't go back to the hotel I was at. As soon as he gets here, I'll text you."

Debbie hangs her phone up and jumps in excitement. "Yes. we got that son of a bitch!"

"If she's being honest, then this might be easier than I thought. If she's lying, we're going to need a backup plan." Elijah massaged his chin in thought. "I think I have the perfect backup plan."

Looking at her keys on the table before taking a sip. "I don't know if it's a smart idea to drive home tonight, but I don't wanna tell Mitch I'm over here. He's going to want to know why, and he has a way of knowing when I'm not telling the truth when I'm drunk."

"Don't worry, you can sleep in the back room. I just changed the bedding yesterday so it's all fresh for you. And I'll call Mitch and tell him that you came over crying all worried about him cheating on you. I'll say that I talked you calm, over too many drinks to drive, so I let you sleep in the back room. Just make sure you set up this meeting after six, so I have time to get my backup plan in motion."

"What is your backup plan?" Debbie asked curiously.

"Oh, don't worry. You'll know it when you see it. I just know Dan's a slick motherfucker." Sucking his teeth. "I bet you he won't be ready for this shit at all." Texting on his phone. "I can't wait until tomorrow."

Debbie holds up her glass towards Elijah. "Cheers to tomorrow."

CHAPTER 19

"We gotta go back! This motherfucker just killed my cousin!" Freddie yelled in frustration to Mitch and Rodney. "Turn the fuck around." Gripping his gun tightly.

"Pull over up there." Mitch directed Rodney. "Little bro, I know this shit is fucked up and you wanna kill the fuck out of Dan right now. Hell, I want you to kill the fuck out of Dan right now. But be real with yourself, do you think us rushing back over there right now is a smart move?"

"I don't give a fuck about being smart. I just want to blow Dan's fucking face off."

"So, you think if we hurry back, that Dan's just going to be sitting there waiting on us? Boy Dan's way smarter than that. If anything, he's somewhere watching to see where we go, so he can ambush us. Nothing we do is going to bring Paul back. And if you get yourself killed then Paul died in vain. Just breathe for the night and I promise you we're gonna get Dan's ass together and I'm gonna let you do whatever you want to that bitch ass nigga."

"Fuck!" Punching his fist into his seat. "I know you're right. I'm just so fucking mad right now."

"Here, hit this." Rodney hands Freddie half of a blunt he had in the ashtray. "That's some shit I got from Paul, so you already know what it smokes like."

"I need this." Pulling his phone out. "I gotta hit my cousin and let him know what's going on."

"Who you talking about? Jack?" Questioned Mitch.

Dialing a number. "Yeah. He's about to be trippin when I tell him. He was just talking to me about if something happens to one of us. How he don't wanna have to tell our moms."

"And then this shit happens." Mitch added.

"Crazy right?" Hearing his phone begin to ring. "Hey cuz. I got some bad news for you."

"What the fuck done happened now? And don't be giving me no bullshit stories." Snapped Jack.

"That hoe ass nigga Dan done killed Paul."

"What the fuck you mean he killed Paul?"

"He tried to set me up earlier using a bitch, but luckily the bitch helped me out of the situation. But I was stranded after I ran off, on foot. So, I had Paul ride with Mitch, and Rodney to come get me. After that, we dropped Paul off at the house and I think he was either already in the house or hiding in the back, but he called me and made me listen to him shoot Paul up. I swear on our grandma's grave that I'm going to kill the fuck out of his ass."

"Where you at now?"

"I'm still in the car with Mitch and Rodney. We just got on the North end. I was about to go over to my chick's house out the Heights."

"Well, I'm making a move right around the corner, so I'm going to meet you out there in just a few seconds."

"Copy" Freddie hangs up the phone. "He ain't trip bad like I thought he was gonna trip."

"Well, if there's anything I know about your cousin Jack, it's that he's a man of action and not emotion. You might think he's taking it well, but I bet you, whoever gets on his bad side won't."

"You've probably got a point because when his brother got shot, it seemed like he didn't even care. Then fifteen minutes later he was shooting up the Gardens and an hour after that he was at the bar buying everybody shots. I think big cuz might be a little bit bipolar. But fuck it. He goes harder and gets more money than anybody I know, besides you." Leaning to look over Rodney's shoulder. "You can just go back in, over there, by the dumpster. My girl stays right in the next building."

"I got you." Rodney backed in and cut off the lights. "I think it's not about being bipolar as much as it's about not letting people see what hurts you. Because that's your weakness. Take what's going on right now for instance. This dirty motherfucker killed Paul because he couldn't get to you. But most of all because he knew that it would hurt you. Now flip the page on him. Who can you get to, that's close enough to him that it would hurt him?"

Freddie looked over at Mitch. "Shit, I don't know. The only person I ever saw him act like he gave a fuck about is the same dude that's paying me to kill him. I never saw him with a girl.

And by the looks of how his girl flipped on him today. That goes to show how close they're not. I don't even know if he got kids or not. What's up Mitch? Who can we kidnap and torture tonight? Who does this motherfucker love?"

"Man, Dan don't give a fuck about nobody. The only person I could say ever meant anything to him was his grandma. After she died, his heart turned cold. I know a couple of broads that he be fucking with, but he ain't gonna care what happens to them. He really is heartless. And that's why I'm trying to get you to play shit smart. You have to expect anything from someone with nothing to lose."

Freddie leaned forward and squinted to see a car coming towards them. "I think that's big cuz right there. He said he was right around the corner. Flash your lights so he knows we're over here. Y'all always in something different. Don't nobody be knowing it's y'all till you pull up."

Rodney looked into Jack's car as he pulled in next to them. "Man, I swear, we might always be driving something different, but Jack always got something different driving." Admiring the dark skin diva in Jack's driver's seat. "I don't know what website he is ordering his hoes off of, but I swear he's a platinum member."

Mitch chiming in. "That boy be buying his hoes on the BOGO deal." They all laugh.

"Boy, y'all too funny. I'm about to hop over here and holler at this fool real quick. Thanks for coming to get me tonight. I almost let this motherfucker catch me slipping. Sorry for nutting up in your ride. I let my anger get the best of me."

"You didn't do anything that wasn't expected. A lot happened tonight. Just be safe tonight and check in with me tomorrow." Mitch dapped Freddie up. "Keep your safety off."

"You already know my shit on go!" Jumping in Jack's back seat next to a pretty, light-skinned girl holding an AK-47. "Damn cuz. Is she big enough to shoot that thing?"

"Oh, don't you worry about my soldiers. All my girls can shoot." Passing a wink to the girl driving. "Ain't that right baby?" Looking at Freddie with a serious eye. "Your girl knows you're out here?"

"Not really, but she knew I was on my way. Why what's up?"

"Let her know you're not coming in tonight. You're about to stay with me tonight. I got a telly out in Youngstown."

"Looking over at the girl next to him. "Is security coming with us too?"

"I don't go nowhere without them."

"Well, since we're gonna be safe. I guess I'll ride."

"That way we can sit down and chill while you tell me what the fuck is going on. These streets are gonna be hot all night after this shit." Noticing the stress on Freddie's face. "You're gonna be alright little cuz. After we get everything out in the air, I'm going to have my Puerto Rican persuasion back there get you right with one of her special body massages. Believe me when I tell you, that girl can do so many other things with her hands, other than hold that gun. If you know what I mean."

"Oh, I understand you completely. And I think that is exactly what I need." Looking out the window into the sky, "This night couldn't be any crazier. I can't believe this dude killed Paul. I'm going to do what you say for tonight and clear my head. Honestly, that's the same thing Mitch told me to do. But in the morning. As soon as I wake up, I'm going to be on a mission to kill Dan's ass. And I'm not relaxing or resting again until I do. And that's on my dead cousin's fresh corpse."

"Amen to that cuz. And I know that you like to make your moves, and you got your own team, but know that I'm out here for all the bullshit too." Assured Jack. "I just told y'all don't let nothing happen to y'all. Now I can't look my big cousins in the face until I deliver the news that this bitch is out of the game completely."

"I just keep hearing his voice in my head yelling out when he got shot the first time, then Dan's voice yelling, do I have your attention? Then a whole bunch of gunshots went off back-to-back. He wanted me to take it personally and it worked. I have to kill this nigga. It's my fault he killed Paul. The only way I can make it right is by spilling this man's blood."

"Like I told you cuz, I'm here if you need me. You already know how I give it up. And if I catch his ass before you do, I'm going to call you on the phone so you can hear me murder the fuck out of his ass. Deal?"

"Deal" Freddie shook Jack's hand.

CHAPTER 20

"Hey Darla, come open your door for me." Dan talked into his phone.

"Where you at? I'm in the door right now." Looking in both directions. "I thought I heard a car out here, so I was peeking out."

"It was me. I'm in the back. Open the side door."

"What do you got going on now?" Darla asked in a sassy tone.

"Man, just open the fuckin door and ask me all these dumb ass questions later. Damn!" Shouted Dan before hanging up the phone. "This bitch is about to make me fuck her up too." Talking under his breath.

"Boy, don't come in here acting all crazy." Holding the door open. "I thought you just pulled to the back of the driveway. Why did you park all the way behind the house like that?"

"Because I wanted to. Why the fuck is you all down my neck for?"

"Why the fuck are you coming over here acting all weird? Parking all in my grass and shit." Looking out her window over her kitchen sink. "You better not have parked on top of my hose either. I just bought that hose."

Pulling some weed and a blunt out of his pocket. "Why don't you make yourself useful and roll this up and give me a chance to think for two seconds before you keep giving me the third degree."

Snatching the stuff from Dan's hand. "You're always talking about I ain't useful, or I ain't good for shit, but every time I turn around you need me for something. All I was doing was making sure your punk ass was okay. I could be like the rest of these thoughtless bitches out here, and not give a fuck about you."

"Sometimes I wish you would." Cocking his head, with disappointment on his face. "I'm starting to believe that you're trying to drive me crazy on purpose. You're always talking about how you wanna be my main chick and shit, but whenever I try to let you do the simplest things to see if you can handle being my broad, all you do is bitch and complain."

"We're gonna see who's bitching and complaining when I make you roll your own blunt with your gimp arm."

"Don't do that to me. I need that blunt so bad right now." Cracking a smile to lighten up the energy. "Don't stand at the counter," kicking the other chair from under the table. "Come sit with me at the table so I can talk to you."

Taking a seat. "So, what's really going on baby daddy?"

"Check this out and tell me am I trippin." Taking a deep breath into his hand. "So, do you remember when I told you I had a shooter bitch to help me with this Mitch situation?"

"Yeah, so what about her?"

"I had her lure in the little bastard that shot me. So, when I got to the spot to put in that work, this bitch pulled out on me."

Darla dropped her jaw in shock. "What the fuck?"

Holding up his finger. "But wait, it gets better. Before I even got there, she hit me to let me know she had him. I specifically asked the bitch was he packing. She says no. I'm like are you sure? And she's like, I'm positive. She says she just watched him tell someone that he didn't need it, which sounded like some bullshit to me. But anyways, while I'm at her neck for pulling out on me, this little motherfucker pulls his shit out on me." Seeing Darla cringe her face up in disbelief. "You look just how I was feeling. Which got me thinking, did these two motherfuckers set me up?"

"It sure sounds like it. I ain't even gonna lie to you." Agreed Darla.

"But if they really did, then I feel like he would've blown my head off." Pausing briefly. "The more I think about it, I think he didn't pull his trigger because she was kinda between us and he didn't wanna shoot her." Trying to show their positions with his hand on the table. "She probably had that boy's mind gone. It's crazy when you see how much power a little bit of pussy has on a nigga. Especially from a bad bitch." Laughing as he continued. "She'd fuck around and have that fool spending all his little weed money on her fresh. Some shit he would never do for an ugly bitch."

"Oh, so she's a bad bitch?"

"You think I'm about to pay an ugly bitch to come all the way down here to lure niggas? I don't think so. I need a sure thing."

"Did you even ask her why she did what she did?"

"Of course, I did. But she more or less brushed it off saying some shit like, he's the little fish. Like we should spare him after he tried to take my whole head off to get the big fish." Pounding his fist on the table. "I want all the fucking fish! Big! Little! I don't give a fuck."

Playing it out in her head. "I gotta be real with you. It almost makes sense." Shaking her head as if she were agreeing with herself. "I mean, Mitch knows who she is. He probably put two and two together from day one. And she probably picked up on that vibe. So, her letting Freddie live might get him to think she flipped sides and turned on you."

"Man, I swear to God, that's exactly what she said."

"Well, that's what I would do. And I'm an ugly bitch. Let you tell it."

"So, I'd be tripping to take her head off? Cause I was about to do that later on tonight."

Looking blown away. "Boy, are you going to kill everybody? Damn! Am I going to be next? Like what the fuck?"

"If I was going to kill your crazy ass, I would've done it a long time ago. Trust me." Pushing her knee. "As much as you piss me off, I probably should've killed you by now. You're lucky you got my little man." Holding his hand like he was pointing a gun at her. "As soon as he turns eighteen though." Making a gun sound with his mouth.

"That shit is not even funny. You seriously gotta stop thinking that killing people is the best way to solve your problems."

"Baby, killing people is the only way to solve my problems." Giving her a wink.

"You are sick."

Dan tried to hug her with his one arm. "Girl you know you love me."

Pushing him away. "No, I don't! Get off me!" Crossing her arms. "Stay serious for once in your life."

"I'm always serious. As a matter of fact, to show you how serious I am, I'm gonna give this bitch twenty-four hours to convince me not to kill her. And if she doesn't, I'm seriously gonna blow her brains out."

"Stop saying that." In a whiny voice. "Just let the girl go home."

"Well, why don't you check her temperature for me?"

"Check her temperature? What the hell are you asking me to do exactly? Cause I don't know what that means."

"Let me slide her through. Chop it up with her. See where her head's at."

Cutting her eyes at him. "And who am I supposed to tell her I am to you?"

Smiling hard. "My sis." Looking at her disturbed face. "What? Would you rather say you're my cousin?"

"What the fuck I look like? Boo Boo the fool?" Furious.

"It ain't even like that, I already told you that I've been rocking with shorty for a little minute now. We put in a lot of work together and she ain't never crossed me, until now." Talking smooth. "If I be honest with you, I kind of trusted the bitch. And for real, the only person I trust more than her is you. So, who better to feel her out for me than you? Believe me, if I had another option, I wouldn't bother to put you out like this. But I really need you or I'm scared that I'm really gonna have to kill her." Looking stern.

Darla just stood there speechless for a few seconds. "I can't believe I'm saying this…"

"You'll do it?" Completing her sentence.

"Yes. I'll do it. I can't have her out here setting up my baby daddy to be killed."

"You see, that's why I fuck with you the long way. These other bitches ain't got shit on you." Tapping her leg. "I know I be pissing you off but you know I'd kill a whole army about you."

"You don't gotta big it up to something it's not. You want me to meet one of your whores so I can tell you whether to keep fucking her or not. That's all this is. So, where is she at now?"

"I got her in a telly in Howland. I figure that will be the last place they look for her. Plus, they know the police are on their shit out there. I doubt if Mitch would risk trying anything out there." Looking down at his watch. "I told her I'm going to have her pick me up in the morning, so I'm going to have her pick me up here."

"Hold up. Who said you were staying the night?"

"Your panties did." Rubbing his hand down the front of her pants.

CHAPTER 21

"Good morning Unc." Joshua greeted Rodney as soon as he opened his eyes. "Moms in the kitchen making us breakfast. Are you going to hang with us today?"

"Nah nephew. I got a lot to do today. But I am going to eat some of that breakfast before I go. What's she cooking anyway? It smells good."

"She said she was making bacon, eggs, and french toast."

"Man, french toast is my favorite." Standing up to fold the blanket he had been sleeping with.

"I think that's why she's making it. She said if anything was going to keep you in the house for a few minutes, it'll have to be covered in syrup." Laughing at his mom's joke.

"You know why I can't always be here with y'all right? Trust me if I could just hang out with you all day and not have to go out to make this money all the time, I'd be the happiest person on Earth. But the way life goes as a grown-up, I gotta get out here and do what I gotta do or I'll starve."

"My mommy's not going to let you starve."

Smiling at Joshua's cleverness. "See, that's the next grown man lesson for you. Any grown man that depends on a woman to feed him is a bum. A man is a man because he handles his business and takes care of his family, not the other way around."

"But what if a man gets married and his wife wants to cook every day? Does that mean that he's not a man if he lets her?"

"He's not a man if she has to buy it and cook it. As long as he's providing the meat, she can prepare it. But just know that if she's doing everything, he's probably going to lose his wife to a man that does something. One thing about relationships, even when you think you got the job of being someone's man on lock, there's always gonna be other guys submitting applications. Your job as a man is never secure. You gotta go hard every day like it's your last because you never know when it might be."

"Well, if I ever get out of this stupid chair, I'm gonna make a lot of money."

"I don't give a fuck if you never get out of that wheelchair, your gonna make money regardless. That wheelchair don't come with an excuse to be broke."

"How am I going to make money if I can't walk?"

"Boy! One of my best friends is in a wheelchair and he's got way more money than almost everybody I know. He even has a dope wheelchair with rims on it."

"You're lying!" Joshua says in disbelief.

"Why would I lie to you? How about I talk to him and set up a day when I can take you to meet him. He might even let you stunt in his wheelchair."

"Are you serious? That would be so cool. Do you think he can teach me how to make money being crippled?"

"I know he can. That's the whole reason I want you to meet him. I want you to see that there is no excuse for you to not be successful."

"So, what does he do?"

"Honestly, I don't even know completely. I just know that he works on computers all day. He has a nice ass house, and a couple of nice ass cars. And a lot of money. So, me seeing him make it the way he is, let's me know that you can make it too. You just need a little direction." Looking down at a message that just came through his phone. "Sorry nephew, I gotta step out and make a call real quick. It's important." Walking past his sister on his way outside. "Good morning sis. You got it smelling good as a bitch in here." Rubbing his belly.

"I was hoping I finished in time so you could eat before you had to leave. I guess I took too long. Huh?" Tina said, with a sad face.

"Nah. I'm just running outside to make a couple of calls real quick. I'll be right back in." Stopping halfway out the door. "As good as that food smells, I would've had to lose my job today before I miss that meal." Dialing Debbie's number as soon as he gets out the door. "What's up Debbie? Is everything okay?" Sounding urgent.

"Everything's fine for now. I just need a favor from you later."

"What kind of favor Debbie, cause Mitch specifically told me that I don't work for you and I'm not trying to fall out with him going behind his back."

Stopping him in mid-sentence. "Look, I know how loyal you are to Mitch and that's exactly why I'm calling you. Now me and Elijah got some shit going on to get Dan up and out of here for good, but Mitch can't know because we need him to just act regular. I've probably already done too much talking over this phone, so what I need you to do later when you drop Mitch off is meet up with Elijah at the address I'm about to send to your phone. And bring Freddie with you."

"And how am I supposed to know where Freddie's gonna be at without Mitch? Hold on." Looking at his phone to see an incoming text. "Never mind. That's Freddie right there." Laughing out loud. "I gotta give it to you. You have picked up well from Mitch. Now I'm really listening. So, the only thing I don't know is, why am I going to tell him that I have to drop him off and leave? Cause that's just not how we move at all."

"I'm going to handle that. I just need you to do this for me. No, fuck that. I need you to do this for Mitch."

"I got you. But if whatever it is that you got planned don't go the way you planned it, just please let Mitch know that I didn't go behind his back on no snake shit. Because at the end of the day my loyalty lies with him."

"Oh, trust and believe, he's going to know by the end of today that you're in his corner one hundred percent. And I know how y'all feel about females doing snake shit and I respect it. To be honest, that's how most of our young men get murdered in the hood. Always through or behind a female. So, I don't blame you for feeling sketchy at first. Like you said, this ain't the protocol. You know Elijah would never play the other side, and this will be the nail in the coffin that will put all this beef to rest. So believe men when I tell you, we do not have any room for error. At all. I wouldn't have even called you if our plan wasn't ironed out. So, are we good or not?"

"We're good. But what time are you talking so I can make sure I'm ready."

“You see, that part I don’t know. We’re kind of playing it by ear. But when it goes down it’s going to happen so fast that you’re going to have to be close by.”

"I can do that. But before I find myself in something I don't wanna be in…"

Cutting him off in mid-sentence again. "Look. I been fucking with Mitch for a real long time, and he’s taught me who to call according to the situation. I know what you do, and I won't ask anything more of you. Just know that my list of people to call is very small. So, if I can't depend on you, then you need to let me know now. "

"You can depend on me. Just hit me and I'll be there." Rodney hung up the phone and just stood still for a moment absorbing the task that he just took on. Questioning himself should he say something at all or roll with the plan. He never dealt with Debbie before, but since he's met Elijah, he sees that even Mitch trusts him with his life. "Y'all better be right." Rodney spoke under his breath as he returned to the house.

"What did you say?" Tina asked after hearing him speak but not understanding what he said.

"Oh, my bad sis. I was talking to myself. I do that sometimes."

"Well, at least you don't answer yourself back." Seeing the guilt on his face. "Or do you?"

Rodney defended himself. "I mean let's be honest here, who really likes to be ignored? Shit, for a long time my voice was the only voice I heard, as much as I was on solitary confinement. I was in that bitch singing to myself and everything."

"Well, I guess it's official. My little brother's crazy. I can just see you now…" Acting like she was hunched over, holding a cane. "Walking down the street, looking old as a bitch. Looking around like, Hey look, there's our friend Mr. Tree. He never leaves his house. Let's go talk to him." Pretending her door was a tree. "Hey Mr. Tree, I told you we'd be back. I was scared that you didn't live here anymore." Busting out laughing at her joke.

“Are you high or something? Because you're clowning!”

“Don’t try and make me out to be the crazy one when you’re walking around having full-blown conversations with yourself.”

“Ma, guess what Uncle Rodney’s gonna do for me?” Joshua says as he rolls in the kitchen.

"What's that?" Giving him her attention.

"He said he's gonna take me to meet his friend so he can teach me how to make money in this wheelchair, so when I get older, I can take care of you."

"That's what he said huh?" Looking over at Rodney. "So, who is this friend that he's talking about? And why am I just now hearing about my son meeting him?"

Clearing his throat. "Well, he's the one I was telling you about the other day. You know, the one behind the donation."

"Oh okay. Well in that case, I think that is a great idea that you go meet him. You never know what you don't know until you try and learn something. So with that being said, be a sponge." Turning back to Rodney. "And when is this meetup supposed to happen?"

"Honestly I haven't even talked to Elijah about it yet. I just know he's gonna be stoked to do it. He likes to do things for people. But I'm going to let you know before I take him around there. It'll probably be sometime next week though." Looking at the display of food Tina had cooked, "We can talk about all that later. What's up with the plates getting put together? I'm starving." Tapping Joshua on the shoulder. "What about you? Are you ready to eat?"

"He's been ready to eat. And thanks for volunteering to make his plate when you make yours. I'm going to get myself together real quick while y'all eat." Tina answered before walking out.

CHAPTER 22

With his feet propped up on the coffee table, Dan texted away on his phone. "Yo Darla, my homegirl is about to pull up. Can you make sure she parks around back where I am?"

Disgusted. "That's your bitch. Bad enough I've agreed to let her come into my house and engage with me. Now you want me to play parking lot attendant for her too?" Posing in front of Dan. with her hip poked out. "See, that's where you got me all the way fucked up."

"You're always tripping. Damn! I just asked you to do it so I don't have to stick my head out the door and let everyone know I'm in here. I swear you do all that yapping and not a bit of thinking. You don't think Mitch might be paying one of your neighbors to watch your house?" Standing to his feet. "Move out the way. If you don't give a fuck about your shit getting shot up, then neither do I."

Pushing him back down on the couch. "I was just playing. Damn!"

Wincing in pain. "You better watch my arm."

"Stop acting like a baby. Your arm wasn't hurting that bad last night." Touching her finger to her chin in thought. "Or this morning the more I think about it."

Watching her sway to the door. "And don't be going rouge with your questions when she gets in here either. Try to have some couth."

"Do you want me to talk to the bitch or not?" Signaling out the door to Passion to roll her window down. "Pull around back honey and park on the other side of Dan's car in the grass." Walking past Dan to open the back door. "I can't believe I let you talk me into this shit. You're so lucky I got love for your stupid ass."

"As long as my stupid ass keeps a roof over your head, you better love me. Now stick to the script."

Opening the back door to let Passion in. "Hi, I'm Darla." offering her hand to Passion.

"It's nice to meet you, I'm Passion."

Ushering her to the living room. “You are a pretty little thing. And your outfits cute. Bro got some good taste.” Admiring Passion’s skintight attire. “Would you like something to drink or eat?”

“Giving off a bashful smile. “I’m not even going to lie, just walking in here made me hungry. It smells like a restaurant in here.”

“Girl, I just whipped up a couple of omelets and some bacon. It was nothing big. What do you like in your omelet?”

Letting out a laugh. “I actually never ate an omelet before. So I guess whatever you put in the one I’m smelling sounds good.”

Placing her hands over her heart. “Oh girl, you don’t even know what you’re in for, but I have one condition.”

“What’s that?”

“Yeah, what’s that?” Dan followed up.

“My one condition is that you gotta come in the kitchen with me and keep me company while I cook.”

“Oh, that’s easy.” said Passion. “I kind of want to know how to make them anyway. Especially if they taste as good it smells in here. I really think God put a fat girl's appetite in my body. I can literally eat all day.”

“Well, if you’re still around you can come over for dinner later.” Setting up her cooking utensils. “I’ll probably make some smothered chicken and rice.”

“Damn girl, you be throwing down.” Passion complimented Darla.

“I gotta feed these hips and thighs before they shrivel away.” Rubbing down her legs. “These may be all I got to get me a husband one day.” Looking back at Passion. “I see you got a little wagon you’re dragging; bro loves him a nice butt. So how did y’all hook up?”

Looking into the living room to see Dan texting away on his phone. Not paying them any attention. “It’s funny you said that, because I was at a bar in Columbus, and he walked up to me and asked me if he could help me carry my load. I thought he was a creep at first, but I gave him my number anyway because he was cute. We hung out a few times and took a couple of trips together. And now I know for sure he’s a creep. But he’s my creep, so it’s cool.”

"So, you really care about my bro?"

"Of course, that's my boo. He just acts like he's too good for claims, so we have yet to put a title on whatever we are. But he knows that I ride for him, that's why he's got me here now." Looking down at her phone, which has begun to ring. "Oh shit! Hey baby, it's Debbie!"

"Put her on speaker so I can listen." Dan said as he walked into the kitchen.

"Hello." Passion says into the phone.

"Hey Angie, this is Debbie. I know you said that you would call me back, but I really needed to talk to you."

"It's all good. So, what's going on?" asked Passion.

"To be honest, I've been thinking a lot about what you said, and I can't blame you for anything. That motherfucker knew he was in a relationship when he had sex with you. I just want to confront his lying ass. I do way too much for that son of a bitch, for him to just act like I ain't shit to him." Fake crying. "I just can't wait to see the look on his face when he sees us both in the same room together."

"Well, just tell me where you want to meet, and I'll come. I don't care. He's been playing us long enough."

"I know you're not from around here, but I'm going to give you an address and you can put it in your GPS and meet me at our house in Cortland at seven. Now you have to be on time because if not I know he'll just walk out. Mitch hates waiting on anyone for anything. Even me."

"I am all too familiar with his impatience. I always just thought he was paranoid. Send me the address and I'll be there."

"I'm sorry to call you in such an emotional state, but I appreciate you agreeing to meet with me. This nigga done fucked over the wrong chick." Concluded Debbie. "If you have any problems finding the house just call my phone."

"I got you. See you at seven." Hanging up and smiling at Dan. "I told you I had it. Now all you have to do is your part."

"Don't you worry about my part. I ain't never had an issue with bodying a motherfucker."

"You're not planning on killing Debbie, are you?" Questioned Darla.

Answering indignantly. "How am I supposed to use her to lure somebody that I'm about to kill, and not kill her? Are you trying to see me locked up?"

"No!" Darla said, defending her actions. "It's just that you know that's my girl."

"Well, your girl is his girl. So, she gotta go. Ain't no ifs, ands, or buts about it."

"I personally don't know her or him. I just know that they're not on team Dan and that makes them the enemy." Passion weighed in.

"Now you see why I fuck with her. You're my whole sis, and you're always tryna take someone else's side."

Pouring her eggs into the pan. "I just don't think you always have to kill everybody. Damn! Can't you just be a grown-up and go the other way?"

"I am. When they go to the cemetery, I'm going to the liquor store. That is the complete opposite way." Snickering at his own remark. "Just chill sis. After this is over today, I promise not to kill anyone else. But Mitch gotta go."

"I guess you gotta do what you gotta do." Adding her ingredients to her omelet. "And you, little miss Passion, what makes you so sure that she's not setting you up? You do know she's a female version of Mitch."

Looking Darla straight in the eyes. "Let's just say that I've been pulling shit off with Dan for a long time now, and I think I'm very good at what I do. And I just know. Besides, I gave her some information that only someone that fucked with Mitch would know. And that's where I think I sealed the deal because before that she wasn't buying it, at all."

"Well, I'm glad that my bro has you on his team. Y'all take care of each other out there."

"Oh, I got him all day." Stated Passion.

"I don't doubt that one bit after meeting you. But I wasn't only talking to you." Clearing her throat. "Bro! Don't let nothing happen to this girl. Do you hear me?"

Standing to put his arm around Passion's shoulders. "Like she said, she's on team Dan, so you know ain't nothing going to happen to her." Walking out of the kitchen. "If something happens to her, I'm killing everybody. And that's on my momma!"

Darla yelled to him as he walked down the hallway. "If something happens to her you better kill yourself because you're the whole reason she's involved with any of this shit in the first place."

"Trust me. I'm good." Fingering through her hair. "I might look like a pretty girl, softy but I was raised with four brothers and three crazy boy cousins that didn't give a fuck that I was a girl. I had to know how to fight and shoot by fifteen. It wasn't until I got with Dan that I actually started to see a profit in using my underlined skills."

"You mean, setting people up?"

"I mean, doing whatever I had to do to make people give me what I want. Whether it's money, information, or even their allegiance. I was good at it from the start. But I have to give it to Dan. He made me great."

Yelling back from the bathroom. "At least someone around here appreciates what I do for them. Hurry up and eat your breakfast so we can make some moves while it's still early."

CHAPTER 23

"You good cuz?" Jack asked Freddie through the door before coming out of his room.

Pulling the cover over his bottom half as he sat up on the pull-out bed. "I'm good, but she ain't." Looking to his side at the tattooed naked body lying asleep beside him.

"She ain't never got no clothes on. I think her parents run a nudist colony in New Jersey or something like that." Handing Freddie a lit blunt.

"Get the fuck out of here. Your bullshitting?"

Raising his right hand. "I bullshit you not. They stay right by a nude beach and every morning they do a naked breakfast and yoga. The shits crazy. Just imagine a big ass open house full of naked bitches stretching and bending and contorting." Gesturing his hands as if he were sculpting clay.

Laughing in disbelief. "So, you did that shit too?"

"Hell yeah, I did that shit too."

"Wasn't there other dudes in there?" Questioned Freddie.

"Of course, there was, but it was like eight of us and like twenty women. I didn't even see those dudes after shit got started. I had tunnel vision like a motherfucker. It's like they do a routine, then for about twenty minutes, everyone does what her mom calls freestyle stretching. So, you got one bitch doing a backbend, one bitch doing splits and another bitch sitting on the floor with her legs over her shoulders, pussy gaped open. And you think I'm looking around to see the woodwork around the room?" Grabbing the blunt and taking a couple of pulls before continuing his story. "I wasn't giving a fuck who was watching me watching them. And the crazy part is, they were all fine as a motherfucker."

"I'm surprised there wasn't nobody fucking in there."

"Her parents are about their business for real. They have a strict no-touching policy. They even say for the females with the other females, that if someone is doing a crazy position that they might need a spotter for, only she and her husband can spot them. They say it's for everyone to feel safe, and I dig it. Cause boy, if only you could see what I'm talking about. I think her mom be hitting on me. She's always calling me some shit like Niño Salvaje. It means wild child in Spanish. And then she'll tell her husband I remember when you were one. Now, I'm not usually a MILF chaser but if you saw her mom next to her you would think they were sisters."

Freddie leaned over to see if she was still asleep. "Bro, you don't think she can hear you?"

Jack gave Freddie a dumbfounded look. "Do it look like I give a fuck if she hears me?" Tapping his ashes on the nightstand. "Besides, it's the truth. And shit. Her little ass might be the most lit all night. Because she be all fucked up and shit. But in the morning this bitch be bottomed out until at least one o'clock. I be having to check her pulse before I leave up out of here sometimes just so my conscience is clear. You feel what I'm saying?"

"That's crazy." Freddie took the blunt and blew a thick cloud of smoke into her face.

"I told you boy." Jack slapped her ass. "Out for the count. But on some other shit. How was that massage?"

"What!" Looking over in amazement at her figure. "When you said she was going to give me a full body massage, I didn't know that meant using her full body. This bitch had me lightweight, turnt out. I was in here slippery than a motherfucker slithering around with her like we were two snakes. I don't know how you do it. But I love what you do big cuz."

"I do what I do for all of us. You always know if you want to eat with me, there's always a seat for you at my table for you and Paul." Balling his fists up and looking in the air. "Fuck! My bad cuz. This shit just got me a little off, but I'm about to be straight. I always told y'all how I'll kill some shit behind y'all, now you finna see."

"I got this cuz. That nigga's going to hell tonight. That's on everything I love. That's why I was even woke when you came in here. I just got off the phone with my peoples. I got this shit in the bag."

"Let me in on it." Insisted Jack.

"I can't this time. But what I can do is let you talk to him before I blaze his ass."

"Oh, you're doing it like that?"

"Straight like that! So, if it's cool with you, I'm just going to hang out here, until like six or six-thirty, then I'm going to have my boy pick me up here."

"You know I got you little cuz." Seeing the pain in Freddie's eyes. "How's your head? Is it in the game? Because you know Dan is about that action, so you gotta stay one step ahead of him at all times."

"Cuz, I'm so slick that he thinks I'm one step behind him when I'm a whole lap ahead of him. It just looks like I'm behind him, but while he's heading towards the curve in the track, I'm heading towards the finish line."

Smiling at his wordplay. "I like how you said that. Maybe you do pay attention when I talk."

"You gotta learn from the best if you wanna be the best. Damn!" Looking up to see two naked bodies in the doorway of Jack's room."

"We were wondering where you went daddy. You and your cousin should come in here and keep us company." Rubbing on the girl next to her before they disappear behind the door closing.

"So, what do you say?" Jack nudged Freddie. "You just said you were going to hang out here for the day, so come hang out. Just watch out for the short dark one. If you think the full body massage was something, she's got a move called the soul sucker. I swear to God if you look into her eyes for even a second while she's doing it, she'll own a piece of your soul forever. I be in the grocery store having fucking flashback visions of this shit. I think her parents were vacuum cleaners or something like that."

"Cuz, you are fucking crazy. Let me throw my pants on real quick."

"Boy, fuck them pants! These bitches ain't worried about your fresh. As soon as I hit that door all my shits are coming off too. You got a long day ahead of you if whatever you got planned goes right, even longer if it goes wrong. At least for a couple more hours, enjoy your life like a motherfucking boss. We can do all that mourning shit later, after Dan's ass is dead too" Jack turned and walked in the room. "Ladies, let's have some fun!"

CHAPTER 24

"This shit's crazy bro." Rodney said to Mitch as he changed lanes on the freeway. "I mean, we dropped Paul off not even ten minutes before Freddie got the call. How the fuck did it go down that fast?"

Covering his face with his hands in frustration. "I've been thinking about that all night and the only thing I can come up with just sounds crazy to me."

"What is it, because for some reason I think we both added it up the same way."

"Shit. How did you add it up?" Mitch asked.

"I keep thinking about that car." Rodney glanced at Mitch to see his reaction.

"Man, that's exactly what I was thinking. On the news this morning they said that the back window was broken and that's where they think the intruder got in."

"And you know he couldn't have broken the window while Paul was in the house because he would've started blasting through the walls or something. He wouldn't have been making no phone calls to Freddie. I'll tell you that." Rodney, building onto what Mitch said.

"Yeah, Paul definitely wouldn't have wasted no time to shoot. Which could only mean one thing, that he was already in the house when we dropped Paul off. And that shit makes me feel so fucked up. But I can't imagine it happening no other way." Letting out a gasp. "That's the only way I can see him getting the drop on Paul like that inside the house."

"Don't trip. We're gonna get that nigga." Assured Rodney.

"I just told them how Dan was and he felt some type of way about that car. We should've all went in with him and made sure shit was straight." Feeling guilty.

"You can't say that. Be honest with yourself, when do we ever walk each other in anywhere? And we're together every day. That type of shit don't even cross your mind because we don't think like that. We all dismissed the car after we didn't see anyone in it. I've never seen Dan drive that car. You've never seen Dan drive that car. So, there was absolutely no way of us knowing that it was Dan's."

"But we all felt it was, that's why we rode down on it." Thinking about what Rodney said in his head. "You're probably right, but I just keep asking myself, what if. You know?"

"Yeah, I know. Like what if we all walked in and it was an ambush? What if it was Dan and a couple of other dudes in there waiting for all of us? What if we all got killed? That would have been checkmate. But it didn't go down like that. Instead, only one person from the team died. And the rest of the team got left to make sure this dirty motherfucker pays for what he did to our homie. I know I said before that I didn't wanna be a shooter, but there's something about Dan that makes me not feel like that anymore. So just know if you need me to point my gun, I will. Gladly."

Mitch pointed at the hotel ahead. "I think this is the one he's at."

Backing in the space. "Tell him we're over by the swimming pool part."

After a few minutes, Freddie came jogging up. "Sorry for keeping y'all so long. I had to get myself together real quick."

"You were supposed to have yourself together before you told us to be on the way." Mitch said, picking at him.

"I did, but the broad was like you smell good… Let me suck your dick again."

"Well, I stand corrected. There's never a bad time for some good head." Mitch said checking himself.

"That boy Jack keep him some hoes, I swear." Rodney said.

"Hell yeah, I had a little Spanish one last night. And she was bad as fuck. But the little chocolate piece I had this morning. Man, she had some moves on her." Laughing out loud. "He told me I was gonna be thinking about her all day long if I looked into her eyes. And my dumb ass did."

"She got him!" Clowned Rodney.

"Hell yeah, she did. I'm over here thinking about going back already and we just got down the street."

Mitch looked at Freddie and grinned. "You're a little whore bag, that's what you are. Just a dog looking for a bitch in heat. You were just thirsting over Dan's set up bitch yesterday."

"And I'm still gonna fuck her ass. Right after I murk her punk ass boyfriend. Just watch and see. I'ma write a book about it. I'm gonna call my shit something dope too. Something like a killer's passion. Y'all better quit playing with me. I'm serious about my shit."

"You're starting to sound like your cousin Jack. Next thing you know, you'll be out here Pimpin hoes too." Mitch looked over to Rodney. "We're gonna have to take this nigga pimp hat shopping."

"Don't forget the cane." Rodney adds.

"Y'all funny with y'alls jokes but I don't know, I just might have to see what that life is like. I mean from how I see it, what's wrong with getting a lot of money while you hang out with bad bitches all day. Then shit, on top of that he's my blood cousin. So, if the game is in him, then it gotta be in me too."

Mitch looked down at his phone. "Damn."

"What's the matter?" Rodney asked.

"It ain't shit for real. Debbie's just finally ready to argue about an imaginary girl I've been fucking. You know the same routine we go through every six months. She'll accuse me. I'll deny it. She'll curse me out. I'll fuck the shit out of her. We'll smoke a blunt. And everything will be okay."

"Looks like you got this down to a science." Observed Freddie.

"After you've been with someone as long as we've been together, a lot of shit pretty much becomes routine."

"I dig it. I don't think I've ever been with anyone for longer than three months. I just don't trust these bitches for shit. They always say we're cheaters. When the whole time they're cheating themselves." Feeling he may have pushed it too far. "No disrespect to your girl or nothing. Evidently, y'all got something way different than the type of relationships I've had."

"I ain't even going to lie, I've been around Mitch and Debbie ever since I first came home, and they got the most wholesome relationship than any couple I know. Even the married people."

"Thanks bro, that's some real shit." Reading another message on his phone. "Shoot me to Elm Road to meet up with her. Then I'm going to have you link back up with me as soon as we're done, so don't go far."

“I ain’t going nowhere. Me and Freddie will probably just go grab something to eat. I’m starving like a bitch.”

“Well, wherever you go, get me something. I haven’t eaten shit since that big ass plate you brought me from your sister’s house. That food was good as fuck.”

“I got you. That’s the last thing I ate too. And you think about it, I had mine before I even brought you yours.”

“Man, I haven’t eaten since yesterday afternoon. Unless you count the pussy, I ate last night.”

“Oh yeah, you’re African kid commercial hungry. Let’s get you some food before your ribs start to show and people start thinking they can feed you for fifty-eight cents a day.” Swerving slightly as he laughed. “You got me about to kill the whole car. But seriously Mitch, how long before you want me to take you?”

“I’m just waiting on her to say she’s ready.” Looking over at the gas station they were passing. “Yo, ain’t that the cop that tried to get me?”

“Where?” Asked Rodney.

Pointing. “Right there, pumping his gas.”

“That sure looks like him.” Agrees Rodney.

“Pull over there real quick.” Taking his gun from his pocket and sitting it on his lap. “Just pull behind his car.” Directed Mitch. “What’s up officer, can I have a word with you?”

“What the fuck!” The officer says under his breath as he walks up to Mitch’s window. “You’re a little way out of your neighborhood, ain’t you?”

“No more than you be when you’re in the hood fucking with us.” Looking down at his gun to make the officer notice. “So, I looked into you pulling me over and there’s no record of a traffic stop that day or any day this month from you. I even checked the scanner transmissions and there was never a call in on my car. So, what type of shit does Dan got you on, because I know you haven’t been handling official police business fucking with me. And more importantly, what do I have to do to make you back off?”

“Well to be honest with you, that wasn’t my issue in the first place. Dan owed my partner Leon twenty thousand from a front he gave him three weeks before our meet-up. He told Leon to bring you the next re-up. You would pay for the last front. Then I was to pull you over and act like you pulled a gun on me resulting in me killing you. That way he would get you out of the way and the dope paid for at the same time. My partner would get his twenty, and I could keep the other ten and the credit for the bust, for lending my hand. So, after you bounced on me, I got cut out of the deal altogether."

"Damn! Well, now you see what happens when you lay with dirty pigs." Looking at him with the side-eye. "So, what would it take to get you to bring Dan to me when you see him again?" Mitch coaxed.

"Well since the going rate was ten in the first place, I'll honor that again."

Mitch popped open the glove box and removed a wad of cash. Counting out ten thousand, he writes his number on the top bill and hands it to the officer. "So, I guess we're in business now."

"That's what it looks like to me." The officer tucked the money and reached out to shake Mitch's hand.

Not responding to the outreached hand mitch turns to Rodney. "Let's get up out of here."

CHAPTER 25

"Go ahead out to the car. I wanna chop it up with my sis real quick then I'll be out." Dan said as he walked Passion to the back door."

"It was really nice to meet you. And if he allows it, I'll see you later for dinner." Passion says nicely.

"It was nice to meet you too. And if not we're gonna have to link up again someday soon."

"If you're cooking, I'm game." Passion anticipated.

"Your girl is so nice bro." Watching her walk outside to the car. "Do not kill that girl. She is literally handing you Mitch on a platter, when you know, you couldn't get to him as easy no other way."

"I feel you. I just don't like loose strings." Peeking out the curtain at Passion in the car. And see this the shit I'm talking about. This bitch is always on her phone. She got me paranoid. Like, who are you reporting to bitch!"

"Do you ever confront her about it?"

"I have, and she always has an answer. But I don't trust her." Sucking his teeth. "If you haven't noticed, I pay her to lie to niggas and set them up all the time. She is the epitome of a liar."

"So, you pay her to be untrustworthy to other dudes. She does exactly that to show you how loyal she is to you. And now you're paranoid that you can't trust her?" Looking stunned. "You're the fucked up one. You have literally created a monster. And it's not that poor little girl out in the car waiting for another chance to prove herself to you, as usual." Waving her finger side to side. "No! It's your mind that you've created a monster of. Your imagination is getting the best of you. You're doing so much to so many people that you're starting to feel like the whole world's out to get you. Now you asked me to talk to her and tell you my honest opinion."

"I did." Agrees Dan.

"And I have sat in this house and hung out with her for hours. I've even paid extra close attention to her interactions with you, even though it was wrecking my mind to watch, but that was only because I saw a woman that genuinely loves your black ass as much as I do. I watched you act heartless with no love for her, the same way I feel you do to me. So, at the end of the day I believe your worst enemy is yourself. It's funny because I don't see you putting a gun to your own head as fast as you're ready to put a gun to everyone else's head."

"How the fuck do you sound? Put a gun to my head. I should put my gun to your head for suggesting some dumb shit like that."

"I wasn't suggesting. I was only observing. Everyone that does something wrong has got to die except for you."

"That's because I haven't done shit wrong. And yes, everybody gotta die. It wouldn't be called the game of life if the flipside wasn't death. It would be called the game of having fun or some bullshit like that. And on the flip side, you would just be bored out of your mind."

Frowning at the smirk on his face. "You are absolutely impossible! I don't even know why you brought her here for me to talk to if you were going to be on the same crap even after I gave you, my opinion. All I'm going to say is, if something happens to that girl, don't come back over here. Your killing people is getting out of control."

"I'm not going to kill the girl. I promise you if she shades me, not only am I going to blow her noodles, but I'm going to bring her back here first and make you watch."

"Get out! I just can't with you no more." Upset.

"We're good. I'm just being honest. That bitch knows how to use her charm as a weapon like a professional. This is your first time seeing her in action. But I'm still going to take your word for everything and I'm not going to do anything to her. As a matter of fact, we'll be back to eat dinner." Turning to make his exit.

"Just remember what I said." Reiterated Darla.

"I got you." Walking out the door. "Who the hell are you out here on the phone with?" Getting in the car.

Holding her phone up. "I'm not on the phone with nobody. I'm on the internet. Why are you always acting like everything's so suspicious?" Questioned Passion.

"Because you be doing some real suspicious shit. Like you haven't looked at your phone in two hours but as soon as you get from around me, you're all in that motherfucker."

"Well excuse me for keeping myself occupied while you say goodbye to your other bitch!" Mumbling. "Talking about she's your sis."

"What the fuck you talking about? That is my sis." Flustered, "Why the fuck would I bring you over here to chill with her all day, if this was my other bitch? You're not even making any sense."

"Okay, now I'm not making any sense. Let's see, all of a sudden I guess I'm stupid and I don't know how to pay attention to my surroundings."

"What are you talking about?"

"I'm talking about the big ass picture of her and her son on the wall in her hallway. So do you want to be honest and tell me why her son looks and smiles exactly like you?"

Laughing off her accusation. "Man, you're buggin. You know what they say about if you feed a kid long enough, it'll start to look like you. Maybe because I'm the main male he sees so he mocks what I do. I don't fucking know. Maybe because I was always pissing her off calling her fat ass through her whole pregnancy. She acted like she hated me. Shit, I don't know! Maybe because he's a black male just like me and people think we all look alike." Running down every stereotype he could muster.

"So, you're gonna keep on lying? I am a female and even if I'm wrong about the picture, I could see how she looks at you. Hell, I could see how she looked at us. Like every time we touched each other, it hurt her a little bit." Looking at him with a dumbstruck expression. "What? You think I can read anybody except for who you don't want me to read?"

Seeing he had nowhere to go in the argument. "I ain't about to do this with you. You're fucking crazy. Let's talk about the issue at hand. Did you pick up the duct tape?" Diverting.

"It's in my purse along with my gloves and my gun. Is there anything else, captain?" Sassily. "I'm just so clueless sometimes. I just need a little guidance."

"Keep fucking trying my patience and see what happens." Raising his hand in position to slap her. "Now I don't know what's gotten into you but you're acting kinda shaky. I need your head all the way in the game. Focus on what we got to do and not what you think I got going on. Cause we can deal with that later."

"Oh, we don't have nothing to deal with later. I'm cool with the whole situation. I'm just glad I got to see that I'm just another one of your bitches that you employ from time to time. I ain't gonna lie, this shit hurts. But you know what they say. No pain, no gain. I grow through everything I go through."

"Well, what's the plan?"

"Really?" Looking at Dan with an evil face.

Jerking at her wheel. "Man, you better watch the fucking road! And yes really, show me that you have your head in the game."

"I'm going to drop you off a few houses down and pull up right past the house. You're going to chill to the side while I knock. When she answers the door, I walk in and act like I'm locking the door, and you're going to storm in past me and lay them down."

"Keep going." Coached Dan.

"I'm going to grab the gloves and duct tape out my bag and tape their hands and feet. After you get the locations on his dope and money, we tape up their mouths and shut them in separate closets. And then we go get the dope."

"What if the dope and money ain't where he says it's at?"

Exhaling heavily before speaking. "Then we go back, and I hold my gun to Mitch's head while you torture Debbie until he breaks."

"And then what?"

"I'm going to tape his mouth back up and you're gonna flip out and act like he's still lying. And you're going to torture Debbie some more, to make sure his story doesn't change."

"And after we get the dope and the money?"

"Then we come back and put bags over their heads and wrap their whole faces in duct tape and let them die in the closet right next to each other. Then we split the bag."

"I like how you added that last part. But I'm willing to do that. We're a team after all, right?"

"That's what I thought we've always been." Rubbing his leg. "Stop worrying. We're gonna go and do the job just like we've done every other job we've ever had to do. And when we're done, we're gonna go somewhere nice and hang out for a week and just treat ourselves like the bosses that we are."

"I like how you said that. But just know that this job is different from any job we ever did, on so many levels. This dude was like my brother."

"So, if you think that you can't kill him because of y'alls bond or whatever, then you walk out and let me handle the business. But it's gonna get handled. And it's gonna get handled today!"

"It's scary how much you're starting to sound like me." Seeing they stopped at a red light, Dan leans over and kisses Passion. "You know you're my baby. This shit just got me stressed out and paranoid because it's too close to home. But as soon as all this is over, I'm going to show you what you mean to me."

Passion smiling. "You promise?"

"I promise."

CHAPTER 26

“Did we come all the way out here to not talk about what we came out here for? I’m confused as fuck Debbie.” Mitch showing his annoyance. “You’re not making any sense.”

A knock came at the door. “Maybe this will make sense to you” Debbie announced as she opened the door.

“Hey, Debbie.” Passions soft voice spoke out. “Let me lock this handle.”

“What the fuck?” Mitch recognized Passion’s voice before he could see her face.

“Get the fuck down!” Dan pushed in right past Passion. “Don’t you even think about grabbing that motherfucker.” Shoving his gun in Mitch’s face. “Get the fuck down on your knees.” Dan grabbed Debbie and put his gun to her head.

“Okay! Okay! Just chill bro.” Dropping down to his knees, with his hands in the air.

“Take his gun and get him taped up.” Seeing Passion struggle with one of her gloves. “Hurry the fuck up, we don’t have all day.”

“I got it.” Passion taped Mitch’s hands behind his back. Then his legs together, before placing a strip over his mouth. Grabbing Debbie’s arm. “Get down!”

“So, it’s like that?” Debbie asked in tears. “Y’all came here to kill us?”

“We came to kill Mitch. You can live if you cooperate, and Mitch does everything we ask. You have my word on it.” Reassured Passion.

“Fuck your word!” Debbie spit in Passion’s face.

Slapping her across the face with a backhand. “Now that wasn’t nice at all.” Pulling her gun out and putting it to Debbie’s head. “Now give me a reason to do it! I’m not going to repeat myself. Get on your fucking knees!” Snatching at her aggressively.

Dan guided Debbie to the floor. “You can’t do shit about it, so stop your squirming” Shouting at Mitch.

“Put your hands together behind your back.” Passion instructed Debbie as she taped her up the same way she did

Mitch. "Who the fuck is that in the driveway?" Hearing a truck backing in.

Dan peeked out the window. "It looks like a moving truck. Y'all expecting company?"

"It's the movers bringing our bedroom furniture." Debbie answers. "If you take this tape off me, I'll tell them to come back tomorrow."

"Bitch you think I'm fucking dumb." Dragging Mitch down the hallway out of sight. "Tape her mouth!" As soon as Passion put tape over Debbie's mouth, Dan drug her in the hallway next to Mitch. "I got this. And if either of you makes a sound, I'm letting everybody have it." Dan tucked his gun in the back of his pants and went to the door to await the mover's knock. "Here they come." Shushing Passion. Knock. Knock. "Who is it?

"We're here to deliver some furniture to Debbie Fisher?" Cracking the door. "There's been some kind of mix up. She doesn't want the furniture delivered until tomorrow."

"Well, she has it scheduled for today. Is she here for me to have a word with?" The mover asked.

Passion crept slow behind Dan and took his gun from behind his waist and put hers to his head. "They said it's scheduled for today. I think you should let them in." Poking the tip of her barrel into the back of his neck.

"Yeah. I think you should back up." The two movers walked into the house, and both pulled out guns. "Go open the back door." Motioning to Passion. "You get that tape off of them." Flipping out his blade and handing it to the other mover."

"I see y'all started the party without us." Elijah said as he rolled in the back door, followed by Rodney and Freddie.

"You didn't think I was gonna miss out on a second chance to have a date with you," Freddie said to Passion who was locking the door behind them. "Now show me we can trust you and hand that over."

Passion placed her gun in Freddie's hand. "You can trust me. I helped make all this possible."

"She's good." Debbie assures as she rubs her cheek.

"I'm sorry if I hit you too hard. I was trying to make it look real."

"Fuck the bullshit!" Mitch stood to his feet. "Passion, tape this nigga up."

"Bitch if you..." Before Dan could get his words out Freddie cracked him across the face with Passion's gun.

"Don't you use that tone with my broad," Freddie demanded. "She with a real nigga now." Signaling Passion. "Go ahead and tape that nigga real good."

"What the fuck is Shawn doing here? And who is this dude?" Mitch asked puzzled.

"You act like you're not happy to see me after all these years." Shawn smiled showing off his gold tooth that replaced his gap as a child. "And this is my cousin Popop. He just wanted to ride with me and get a piece of the action."

Giving everyone their proper greetings. "Boy y'all got here just in time." Mitch kicked Dan in the stomach. "This nigga almost had me checked out of here."

"So how about I check him out!" Popop pulled a sawed-off shotgun out of his bag, cocked it, and placed it against Dan's head.

"Woah! Woah! Big boy." Mitch put his hand up to stop Popop from blowing Dan's head off.

"I'm not going to shoot until you say the word." Popop stared Mitch fiercely in the eyes to instill fear.

"You can't shoot no big ass cannon like that in this type of neighborhood. These white folks will have the police lined up the block before we can get our black asses out of the driveway. You Norfolk niggas is crazy!"

"No disrespect fam, but I ain't no Norfolk nigga. I'm from South Norfolk. It's totally different." Laying his shotgun on the counter and pulling a three eighty out of his pocket and aiming it at Dan's head. "Is this better?"

"No, that's not better." Humored by Popop's intensity. "Hey Shawn, tell your man to stand down. I want my guy to kill him. He's already been paid for the job."

"Yo buddy don't squeeze on that pussy nigga. I guess we just came for security." Directed Shawn.

"I wouldn't say all that," Elijah said cracking his knuckles. "Now my cousin has a point, Freddie has been paid for the job. But I personally don't think a quick death is enough for our dear friend Dan. So, what do you say? I'll give you thirty minutes to have all the fun with him as you like. You can do anything but kill him."

"I'll give him an hour." Mitch upped Elijah's offer. "Stop your squirming. There's nothing you can do to stop this." Mitch mocked Dan. "Freddie, set your watch and when he gets down to his last ten minutes give him a sign to start wrapping it up and then you do your part. But no guns." Mitch points to a set of knives on the counter. "And make sure everything y'all do is on the plastic."

Passion interrupted. "I don't mean to undermine your plan or anything, but I would like to give you a suggestion."

"Speak up." Mitch accepts.

"Well to minimize the sound and blood spill you should put a bag over his head and take that duct tape and tape his head up like a mummy, making sure to tape his mouth and nose extra tight and let him suffocate himself. I mean, that's what he was going to do to y'all."

"That's how you were going to take me out?" Kneeling beside Dan's head. "I thank you brother for such an elaborate idea." Tapping him in the forehead with his gun. "You heard the lady, Freddie. Make this nigga a mummy when Popops done."

"You should wear these when you handle the tape. If you didn't know, tape has a way of holding your fingerprints." Passion handed Freddie the pair of gloves she had for Dan. "Popop."

"What's good momma?"

"Can you do me a huge favor please?" Lifting her shirt to expose a big bruise on her stomach. "This motherfucker punched me so hard in my stomach that I think he may have cracked my rib. Can you show me what it looks like when a real man punches a man in his stomach? Because I only saw the move work on me, but I'm just a little old girl." Taunting Dan as she speaks.

"My pleasure." Popop stronged Dan to the floor on his back and choked him with his left hand, while repeatedly punching him in his stomach with his right hand. "We're gonna have us some fun tonight!"

"Should I be timing this?" Freddie asked.

"Nah. This is just the pregame." Mitch turned to Rodney. "You good? You've just been standing over there quiet since you came in here. You wanna wait in the truck? This shit is about to get real in here."

"I told you I'm on a whole new level. I'm ready for this. I've just been taking it all in."

"Okay. Then help Freddie lay the plastic over the kitchen floor." Looking around and seeing how organized everything was. "So how were y'all planning on getting his body out of here?"

"That's the point of the moving truck and mover uniforms." Elijah began to break it down. "They're gonna wrap him in plastic. Then fold him up in your couch bed. After that, they're going to take all this furniture out of this front room with them."

"To where?" Inquired Mitch.

"Well, my cousin has a pig farm in Pennsylvania. So, we're gonna stop by there and deliver the couch." Shawn joined in. "Shit we might just deliver all the furniture if he wants it. Then we're gonna watch him cut that niggas body up into small sections before tossing his body out to the pigs. Then we'll clean the truck out and go back home as if none of this ever happened." Reaching his hand out to Elijah. "I know this doesn't make us even for what happened to you behind my beef, but I hope this does something to my debt."

"Brother we were good the day I woke up at the hospital and you were there with me, and I told you we were good." Shaking his hand. "Thank you for coming through."

"Well, since everything is going according to plan." Tapping his wrist to Freddie. "You can go ahead and start that watch."

ACKNOWLEDGMENTS

I can't let this project be complete without personally thanking all of you for believing in me enough to read my book. I hope I have met your expectations and I ask that you continue to support me in the future. It's only going to get better from here.

Follow:
Instagram: @visualwording
E-mail: glogantheauthor@gmail.com

www.ingramcontent.com/pod-product-compliance
Lightning Source LLC
LaVergne TN
LVHW020639100826
845148LV00012B/2247

* 9 7 8 1 7 3 7 0 6 7 6 0 3 *